SWORN TO MURDER

SISTER DIANE CAROLLO

SR. DIANE CAROLLO

Sworn to Murder

A Sister Maggie Mystery
Book 2

sisterdianecarollo.com

Ottawa Press and Publishing Mystery (OPP Mystery)
ottawapressandpublishing.com

ISBN 978-1-988437-68-2 (softcover)
ISBN 978-1-988437-63-7 (epub)
ISBN 978-1-988437-64-4 (mobi)

sisterdianecarollo.com
Cover Design: Mystery Cover Designs/Indie Book Designer
Interior Book Design/Formatting: Mystery Cover Designs/Indie Book Designer

Editor: Joanna D'Angelo

Published in Canada

CONTENTS

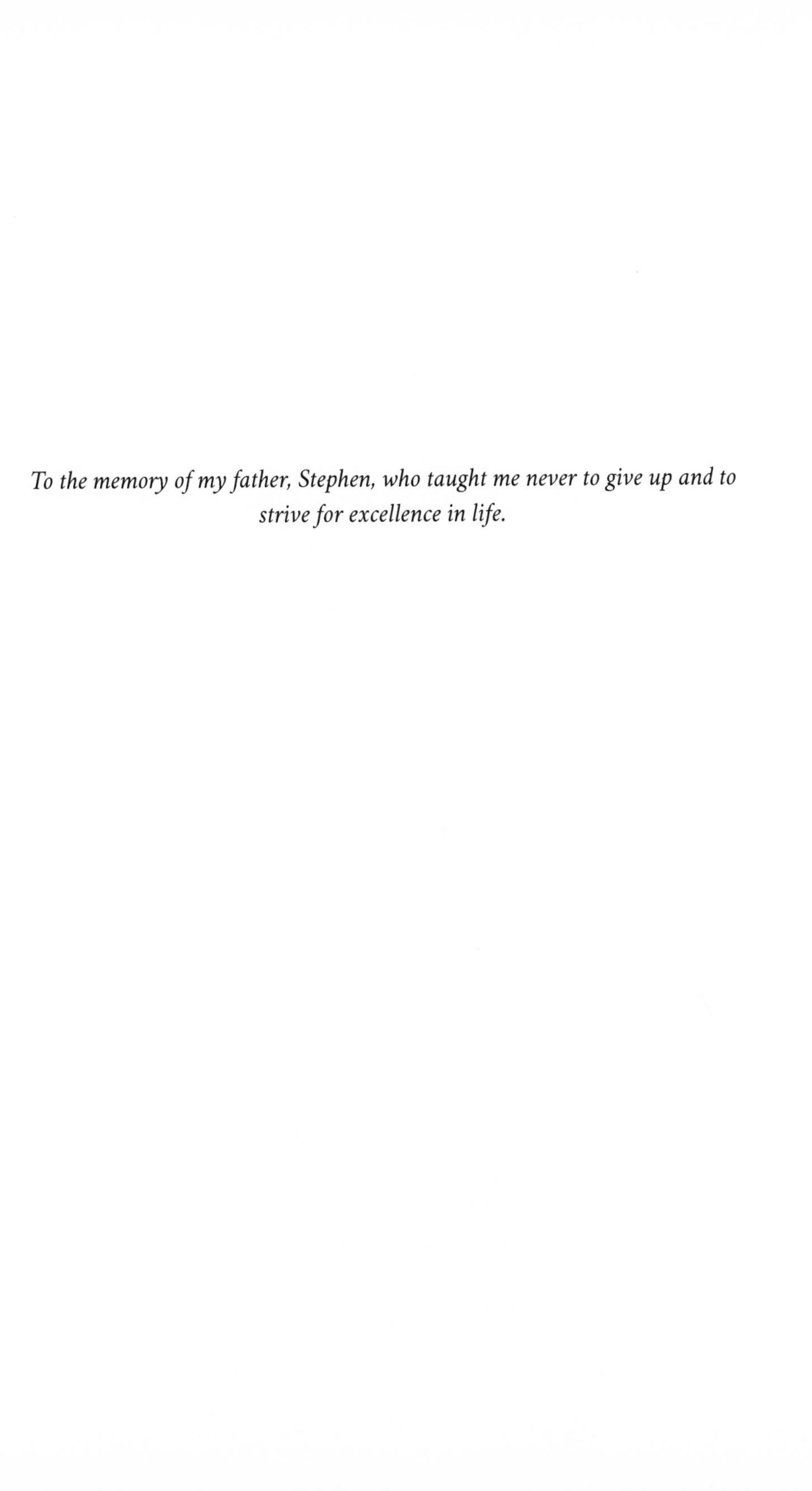

To the memory of my father, Stephen, who taught me never to give up and to strive for excellence in life.

ACKNOWLEDGMENTS

My heartfelt thanks to Joanna D'Angelo, Editor, Author, Publishing Coach, and Promo Gal, for encouraging, guiding, and inspiring me to keep Sister Maggie ever present in the exciting world of fiction. And thank you to Amy Sharp, a truly sharp copy editor with a flair for fine-tuning. I also wish to thank Teri Barnett of Mystery Cover Designs/Indie Book Designer for her clever cover and lovely book design. A special thank you to my new publisher, OPP Mystery and Ron Corbett.

A special thank you to Dr. Robert Shumaker, President of the Indianapolis Zoo, for his dedication to conservation, preserving the future of our planet and its biodiversity. In a special way, I'd like to thank Dr. Shumaker for allowing me to meet Rocky, the orangutan, who was the inspiration for Leo in this book.

PROLOGUE

April 2, 1991
Danfield College
Danfield, Indiana

"YOU CAN'T JUST WALK AWAY from us. That makes you a defector and a traitor to the cause," Jared Taylor said as he shoved Sam Browning against the wall of his dorm room.

Trapped in the tiny space with Jared and two more members of the Alliance of Heritage Nationalists, Sam tried to breathe through his fear. His effort failed when the guys watching the exchange stared at him with blank expressions. When he joined the group, he'd had no idea it would mean life or death.

"That tattoo—" Taylor pinched the ink on Sam's arm "—means you're loyal to the AHN." Taylor's pale blue eyes held a warning.

Sam knew how violent Jared could become, especially after seeing him throw a classmate to the ground and beat the boy's face bloody. The student's only offense was voicing an opinion that some ignorant white guys proved to be on the wrong side of history when they embraced the ideology of white supremacy. Taylor's cousin, Mitchel

Fowler, had pulled him off the student. The same Mitchel Fowler who now leaned forward and poked Sam in the chest.

"You said being one of us was in your blood," Fowler snarled.

Dylan King, the leader of the campus group, crossed his arms. In a calm voice, he said, "If you don't believe in the scientific evidence that proves the superiority of white people over all other races, then you don't deserve to be part of our noble organization." The other two goons stepped aside as Dylan strolled up to Sam and regarded him with a cool green gaze. "I saw you talking to that 'African-American' girl the other day on campus." He used air quotes and sneered as he used the correct term in a sarcastic voice. "Does she have anything to do with your decision to abandon our cause?"

Sam shifted along the wall to give himself space to think. If only he could get to the door, he could make a run for it. He managed to take a couple of steps but tripped on his sneakers. *Darn my own clumsiness.* "She was only asking for directions to Spratt Hall," he sputtered, regaining his balance. "Look, no hard feelings, but I realized I need to focus on my studies."

"Nice try," King said with a smirk. "Since when did you go all nerdy?"

"Yeah," Taylor echoed. "Besides, the AHN is about assisting its members when necessary."

"You mean cheating."

King shook his head. "Haven't you learned anything from us? AHN is all about helping our fellow members get top scores and then primo jobs after we graduate."

"Yeah, because we're tired of outsiders taking our jobs," Fowler said. "Or have you forgotten?"

"I-I just don't see the point of violence," Sam said, trying to remain calm. His legs trembled, but he figured he'd be better off if he was honest. "It doesn't accomplish anything." There. He said it. Sam's gaze took in all three men. King had short blond hair and blue eyes. While Fowler had brown wavy hair and brown eyes, Taylor was balding and had a buzz cut that made his pale eyes look all the more menacing.

"Sometimes violence is necessary to make a point," King said as he stepped back and gestured to Fowler with a slight nod.

Fowler grinned as he lunged at Sam and delivered a powerful punch to his jaw.

Sam stumbled back, grabbing onto the bookshelf to keep from falling. Books tumbled to the floor as Taylor yanked Sam by his sweatshirt and pushed him down. King delivered a hard kick to Sam's side. Sam groaned and clutched his ribs, the pain so sharp he feared they'd cracked.

Three loud knocks sounded on the door. "What's going on in there? Open up!" a voice called out. The door suddenly opened, and Residential Assistant Mikel Obi, known on campus as Mike, stepped into Sam's dorm room, master keys in hand. His gaze went straight to Sam, who was still on the floor, holding his side.

He turned to the three men who stood over Sam and stared at them with narrowed eyes.

Sam attempted to smile, but it turned into a grimace. "Everything is fine, Mike. W-we were j-just horsing around, and I t-tripped."

Mike turned to the three hoodlums. "I think it's time you gentlemen leave before I report you to the head of the housing office." He offered Sam a hand up.

The three thugs exchanged glances and made their way to the door. King sneered at Sam. "Try not to be so clumsy in the future." He scowled at the six-foot-seven-inch resident advisor from Nigeria. "Let's get out of this cesspool," he said.

After they'd left, Mike shook his head at Sam. "What's going on? What have you gotten yourself mixed up in?"

Sam held his side as he made his way to the unmade bed and sat with a groan. He rolled up his sleeve and showed the RA the Valknot tattoo identifying him as a member of the AHN. Mike raised his eyebrows. "I've seen that symbol around campus, mostly graffiti. It's connected to the AHN, right?"

"The Valknot is also known as the *knot of the slain*," Sam replied. "It's an old Norse symbol associated with the afterlife. Three intertwined triangles. White supremacists who have this tattoo are willing to die for the cause. I just told those guys that not only was I not willing to die for the cause, I was quitting the group."

Mike crossed his arms over his muscular chest. "They preach pseudoscientific arguments that support white supremacy. They use a corrupted form of religion to preach hate."

"I know," said Sam. "I'm sorry, Mike."

"As a Nigerian with dark skin, they consider me worthless trash. Why did you join them? I know you're not a racist. It makes no sense."

Sam blew out a breath. "I was going to tell you later today after I told King and his goons that I wanted out. Let me explain. Please."

"Okay." Mike sat in Sam's desk chair, his mouth set in a thin line, his eyes reflecting disappointment.

Sam didn't blame his friend for feeling betrayed. But he had to explain. "You know my kid brother was murdered by an illegal, right?"

Mike nodded.

"So that was four years ago. His death really kicked me in the gut, especially because Nathan and I did everything our folks said was right. When you do the right thing, you're safe. Safe and saved. But they were wrong. Nate wasn't safe, so they must have been wrong about everything."

Sam twisted and moaned. "Hey, Mike, can you reach the top right desk drawer? I think I have some aspirin or something in there."

Mike rummaged around the desk drawer and found the aspirin. He handed Sam the pills and a bottle of water from the small fridge. "So you figured if one immigrant is a murderer, all immigrants are murderers?" Even with the musical accent, Mike's voice was dry as dust.

"C'mon, dude, just listen. My brother's death ruined my parents' marriage. Then my girlfriend dumped me my first year of college for some rich Egyptian exchange student. She even converted to Islam so they could get married."

"Life is tough."

"You wear sarcasm like it's your favorite t-shirt, bro."

Mike's slight smile was the only response.

"Anyway, my life took a nose-dive to hell," Sam said with a crack in his voice. "No more going to Church, no more wanting to follow rules or laws. And I started drinking all the time.

"I met those guys at a bar in town that doesn't really check IDs. They seemed cool, so we hung out all night. They drove me back to campus, but I was so wasted I couldn't remember how to get back to my room. They let me crash in their dorm."

Sam shook his head as his face heated with shame. "At first, I was drawn in by their loyalty to each other. They called it 'allegiance.' I liked that they talked about honor and respect. They wanted to know about my past. They sympathized with me and said what happened to me was unfair, but it kept happening everywhere to guys like us. Over time, they convinced me the country was going down the tubes because of immigration and minorities." Sam paused and rubbed the tattoo on his forearm. "I started to believe them. They said the AHN was about sticking up for each other, and they reeled me in. Look, I just wanted to feel whole again, to have friends who had my back. To belong to something that would take away the pain. Pretty stupid, huh?"

"You could have joined a fraternity," Mike said with a raised eyebrow. "But the AHN? It's like the mafia. They won't leave you alone as long as you're at Danfield."

"I know that now." Sam winced as he touched his aching jaw. "Since the spring semester ends in two days, my plan was to leave early tomorrow morning." He reached down and pulled his packed suitcase from under the bed. "I'm transferring to Danvers College in Indianapolis for the summer session. They've accepted all my credits. By the way, how did you know the guys were in my room?"

"Your roommates found me. They told me you were getting your ass kicked and needed help."

"King told my roommates to get lost. I don't blame them for taking off." Sam shrugged and rolled his eyes at his own stupidity.

"Thanks for your help, dude." Sam used the sleeve of his sweatshirt to wipe his bleeding lip. "I'm glad you showed up when you did."

Mike reached into the pocket of his red and white tracksuit pants and pulled out a handkerchief. He handed it to Sam. "You have been a good friend to me this semester when I started as an RA. No self-respecting white supremacist would do that. I know you're a good guy, Sam. You went through bad stuff and let those guys manipulate you. Always stand up for what you believe. I have been doing that my whole life."

Sam nodded. Mike was a track and field athlete and a campus superstar. He was training for the upcoming Summer Olympics in Barcelona, Spain. Not only was he studying with a full scholarship in engineering, he was a teaching assistant in addition to his RA job. He was graduating early and then heading to Spain to train full time before next year's games. Sam and his roommates were a little in awe of Mike.

"Be careful, Sam," Mike warned. "Those lowlifes hunt in packs. They will come back later tonight or early tomorrow to beat you to a pulp. You need to get out of here and off-campus by this afternoon. I'll drive you to the bus station if you want."

"Why are you doing this for me?" asked Sam.

"Do you know much about Nigeria?" asked Mike.

Sam shook his head. "Only a few things you told me." Mike hadn't seemed open to talking about his childhood in Nigeria, and Sam never pried.

"My birth country has its share of terrorists and tribal violence. As an Igbo, I belong to the third-largest ethnic group in the country. Other ethnic groups hate the Igbos. My father, Marobi, ran a successful automotive parts business with his brother Ikem. My father and Uncle Ikem and Ikem's son, Jamal, were murdered by jealous members of the Yoruba tribe when I was a boy."

Mike clenched his fists. "My mother feared for my safety as heir to my father's business. She sold the business, and we fled Nigeria. She asked for help from her oldest sister, Adanna, who is a citizen of the United States. My aunt had studied here and married an African American physician named Arthur Whitaker. We lived with them in Danfield until my mother found work. Eventually, we became citizens and never looked back." Clearing his throat, Mike continued. "As a child, I could do nothing to prevent the deaths of my father, uncle, and cousin, but I can help you avoid becoming a victim of the AHN."

..*.

Danvers College
One Month Later

Sam stopped by the Student Union Building to grab a coffee before he went back to the library to finish his essay. He picked up the Indianapolis newspaper on the couch and was shocked by the headline: *Track and Field Olympic Hopeful Found Dead. Mikel Obi, a senior at Danfield College who was expected to lead the U.S. track team at the summer Olympics, was identified today as the man killed in a car crash near the campus. Following his graduation later this month, Obi planned to train in Europe for the Barcelona Olympics, according to Danfield track coach Jim Beamer. "He was a gentleman, straight-A student, and a star athlete—destined for great things," Beamer said.*

Police said Obi lost control of his car and veered off the road Monday night, crashing into a tree. He was later pronounced dead at the hospital. The college will hold a memorial service for Obi this coming Friday in the college chapel. Condolences may be sent to the family in care of the Paragon Funeral Home.

Sam read the tributes from other students, faculty, and coaches. His eyes blurred with tears. The article had also stated there had been a flash rainstorm the night of the accident, implying that the weather may have factored into the crash. Sam wondered if King and his cronies had been the real factor behind the accident. Maybe they had done something to the car or to the road to cause the crash. Obi was an expert driver, never drank or did drugs. No way he would have lost control and smashed into a tree—rain or no rain. Sam thought for a moment and remembered something about Mitch Fowler and his cousin Jared Taylor. They often boasted of their mechanical skills, especially with cars. Sam figured one or both of them had rigged Mike's brakes to fail.

Mike had saved Sam's life from King and the AHN, but sadly, Sam couldn't do the same for Mike. He thought about going to the police and telling them his theory, but with no proof, what would it accomplish? And the AHN might come after him as well. Sam wiped his eyes, wishing he'd never joined that horrible group. The only thing he could do was finish school and try to make a difference in the world. He would do it for Mike. He wasn't sure what he should do, but he knew that in time, he would figure it out.

CHAPTER ONE

April 15, 10:30 a.m.
Present day
Our Lady of Guadalupe Convent
New Hope, Indiana

"BUT I DON'T SNORE. I hate the idea of using a breathing machine at night," Sister Mary Ruth, complained.

"The sisters and I have to disagree. You definitely snore," Sister Maggie Donovan said as she drove Sister Mary Ruth back to Our Lady of Guadalupe Convent from the medical supply store. "I won't say who, but a few of the sisters have threatened to put tents up in the back yard with sleeping bags."

Sister Maggie stifled a chuckle. Sister Mary Ruth, who was called Sister Ruthie for short, was one of the most loving and kind-hearted people Sister Maggie had ever known—and the most stubborn. Sister Ruthie's medical issue was no laughing matter, but her stubbornness and the reaction of the sisters to her snoring bordered on comical.

"Oh, that's just nonsense," huffed Sister Ruthie.

When the technician had handed Sister Ruthie the black case

containing the CPAP machine, Sister Maggie, who'd been looking at motorized wheelchairs for her mother, overheard the elderly sister whisper to the woman that she didn't need or want the machine, but was told she had to use it by her superior. Sister Maggie raised her eyes heavenward.

Despite the medical report on her sleep apnea, Sister Ruthie insisted the CPAP machine was an exaggerated response to her snoring.

Sister Maggie didn't tell the elderly nun that Sister Mary Felicia's parents offered to lend them their old RV so the sisters could get a good night's sleep. She also didn't mention that Sister Rose Marie had suggested Sister Ruthie be the one to sleep in the RV. Sister Maggie turned up the air-conditioner in the car. It was a sweltering ninety degrees outside, contradicting the weather forecasters' prediction for a cooler June day.

"I can't fathom how that sleep gizmo will make any difference." Sister Ruthie reached for a tissue and blew her nose with a great honking sound.

"Your snoring has been described by some to be akin to a buzz saw," Sister Maggie replied. "Do you forget what Dr. Trippi said at your follow-up appointment? Your sleep test showed that you need the machine because you stop breathing frequently during the night. That CPAP machine—what you call a gizmo—will force air into your lungs throughout the night, remedy your snoring, and restore sanity to the sisters at Our Lady of Guadalupe Convent."

"Well, I suppose I could get used to it if it means bringing peace back into our midst."

Sister Maggie pulled into her parking spot and smiled at the older nun. "Thank you, Sister Ruthie. I knew you would do what was best for all concerned. Imagine how rested you will feel when you wake up in the morning."

"It will be nice not to fall asleep during morning Mass," Sister Ruthie said.

"Indeed, a bonus if I ever heard one. Sister Maggie hid a smile as she got out of the car. The two nuns were greeted in the front hall with great enthusiasm by the other sisters. The group made their way to the kitchen and out the back door where a picnic was laid out under the shade of the maple tree.

"Well, isn't this splendid," Sister Maggie declared, winking at Sister Mary Felicia.

"It was such a lovely day, warmer than expected," Sister Mary Felicia said. "Perfect for a picnic. Besides, it's very comfortable under this tree, wouldn't you say, Sister Ruthie?"

"Indeed, it is. I do love this tree, but I don't think I would have liked sleeping under it at night," Sister Ruthie said.

"Whatever do you mean?" Sister Rose Marie asked, setting a bowl of potato salad on the picnic table.

"Now that I have a CPAP machine, I won't be bothering anyone anymore with my snoring, and I can enjoy the lovely view of this tree from my window at night rather than gazing up at it from my sleeping bag."

"Sister Ruthie, we would never have allowed you to sleep out here," Sister Mary Frances declared, filling their glasses with iced tea. "*We* would have slept out here instead."

Sister Mary Felicia laughed out loud. She was joined by Sister Rose Marie and Sister Mary Frances. Sister Maggie glanced at Sister Ruthie, whose lips had begun to twitch. Soon they were all enjoying a good laugh as they tucked into their picnic lunch.

Sister Mary Felicia's cell phone buzzed. Picking it up, her eyes lit up as she texted back and then turned to Sister Maggie with a big smile. "Guess what?"

"What?" Sister Maggie asked, taking a bite out of a big, juicy strawberry.

"My cousin Jaime Bauer, the new events director for the Indiana State Zoo, just texted me he can take us on that special tour of the zoo tomorrow morning."

"That's great news," Sister Maggie said. "You must be happy to have Jaime working so close by. He was at the New York State Zoo for quite a few years wasn't he?"

"Yes, I'm thrilled. Everyone in the family is. It's a great promotion.

He's worked really hard over the past ten years," Sister Mary Felicia said. "By the way, Jaime is arranging for us to meet Leo the orangutan." Sister Mary Felicia's eyes danced.

"Oh, that is definitely wonderful news," Sister Maggie said. "I can't wait."

"Who's Leo?" Sister Rose Marie asked as she brushed a fly off her blue tunic sleeve.

"Leo is the newest resident of the Indiana State Zoo."

"Resident?" asked Sister Mary Frances.

"He's an orangutan," said Sister Mary Felicia, taking a bite of her ham sandwich.

"You mean all this excitement over going to see a gorilla?" Sister Ruthie shook her head.

"Leo is not a gorilla, Sister Ruthie, he's an orangutan. There is a difference," Sister Mary Felicia said.

"What's the difference?" asked Sister Mary Frances.

Sister Mary Felicia turned to Sister Maggie. "Go for it."

Sister Maggie smiled. "I'm glad you asked that question, Sister Mary Frances. For starters, gorillas are the largest ground-dwelling primates and come from the forests of central Sub-Saharan Africa. Orangutans, with their reddish-brown hair instead of the brown or black hair of gorillas, spend most of their time in trees and are currently found only in the rain forests of Borneo and Sumatra. They are native to Indonesia and Malaysia. Except for humans, orangutans are also the most intelligent of the primates."

"Sister Maggie, I have never known anyone who is as curious about everything as you are," Sister Rose Marie said with a chuckle.

"The world is full of wonders, so why not explore them? Who wants to join us tomorrow?"

"Shannon, my niece, is coming by tomorrow to take me to lunch," replied Sister Ruthie.

"I have an early afternoon meeting to attend at St. Luke's Hospital," Sister Rose Marie said. She worked as a nurse practitioner in the community.

"And I have an end of the year luncheon planned with this year's catechists," declared Sister Mary Frances, the religion director for the parish.

"Well, you three will be missing a grand tour," Sister Maggie said, popping another strawberry into her mouth.

CHAPTER TWO

April 16, 11:00 a.m.
Indiana State Zoo

"THERE'S my cousin Jaime and Bob Souter, the zoo director. They're waving to us," Sister Mary Felicia said as she waved back.

Sisters Maggie and Mary Felicia headed to the zoo entrance where the two men stood.

"Hm...Souter looks a bit like Richard Gere," Sister Maggie mused. "And Jaime resembles Robert Pattinson, that young actor who played a vampire."

"Sister Maggie, you notice everything, don't you?"

"Why, thank you," Sister Maggie said. "When you come from a family of cops like I do, you develop an eye for detail."

"Well, I am ever thankful for your eye, Sister Maggie."

Sister Maggie smiled at the young nun, who had been through a lot in her life. After winning a nationwide singing talent contest as a teenager, the then Casey Bauer quickly rose to fame and fortune. During a tour break, while she was in New York, a deranged photographer caused her limousine to crash, killing both her little brother

Joshua and the driver, Benny Lopez. This led Casey to several years of depression, counseling, and soul searching until she finally discovered her purpose in life. She asked to be admitted to the religious community known as the Adorers of Divine Love and seemed to be fulfilling her destiny.

"All aboard," Bob said a few minutes later as he and Jaime helped Sisters Maggie and Mary Felicia into the six-seat golf cart provided for their tour. A short distance away, Jaime stopped the vehicle to pick up Charlie Wells, who had just emerged from the administration building where both men had their offices.

"Meet Charlene Wells, better known as Charlie. She's the other orangutan zookeeper who uses sign language to communicate with Leo. She and Sam Browning are part of the research team studying language and communications skills with apes," Bob Souter explained.

The tall, slender young woman wore beige shorts, a green polo shirt, and had a walkie-talkie clipped to her belt. She gave Sisters Maggie and Mary Felicia a bright smile as she slipped into the seat across from them. Sister Maggie thought the zookeeper was stunning and could have been a model. Her long black hair was pulled back in a ponytail. It swung back and forth like silken threads as she moved. Her light green eyes sparkled in the sun.

"My pleasure to meet y'all," Charlie said with a southern accent. "Sam is already with Leo having a chat." Charlie added that Leo knew one hundred and fifty modified American Sign Language words and phrases, and had created a few of his own signs that Sam Browning called Ape Sign Language. "I'm still learning their secret words and expressions," joked Charlie.

A few minutes later, the zoo cart stopped. Less than twenty feet away, a man and an orangutan gestured to each other through the fence that separated them.

"That's Sam and Leo," Charlie said.

Sister Maggie smiled at the fascinating gestures both man and animal were signing to each other. Behind Leo stood a ladder the orangutans used to climb up to a platform station at least thirty feet above ground.

"I think Leo will be delighted to have visitors," Jaime said as he helped Sister Maggie out of the golf cart. He then introduced Sister Maggie to Sam. Sister Mary Felicia smiled and greeted Sam with a hug since they had met before numerous times.

Sister Maggie spotted a wince on Sam's face, then it was gone. She wondered if he'd been hurt recently—perhaps at work—but decided not to ask about it. Sometimes it was best not to ask a question unless you already knew the answer.

"A pleasure to meet you, Sister Maggie," Sam said. He smiled at Sister Mary Felicia. "I'm sure Leo will be eager for you to sing to him again."

Bob strolled up to the fence. "Leo is probably not eager to see me or hear my voice," he said. "Earlier this morning, he asked me for a meat-cheese-bread, better known as the Stack Five Burger. I told him he couldn't have one because he'd had one last week. Unfortunately, some of his caretakers in the past spoiled him by indulging him a little too often."

Charlie raised one eyebrow. "That's why Leo calls you Stink Man."

The zoo director cleared his throat. "I'm happy to be known as Stink Man if it means Leo stays healthy. Those Stack Five Burgers from Burger Heaven should only be an occasional treat for Leo and should never be part of a regular diet. Everything in moderation. Just as that rule applies to humans, so it applies to animals," he added arching his heavy brows.

"Agreed," chimed in Jaime and Charlie at the same time.

Sister Maggie did agree in principle, although she couldn't help but feel for Leo. She had a hard time resisting the Double Cheesy Jalapeño Burger at Burger Heaven, her favorite fast food restaurant in town. *Hm...I haven't been there in months,* she mused. Sister Maggie's attention was brought back to the orangutan.

Leo's eyes were fixed on Sister Mary Felicia. "Leo is staring at you," Sister Maggie said.

"He also gave you the once-over," the young nun replied.

Sam laughed. "Sister Mary Felicia and Leo are old friends. He enjoys it when she sings to him."

“What do you sing to Leo?” Sister Maggie asked.

“Oh, just a little nursery rhyme,” Sister Mary Felicia replied as her face flushed.

“What nursery rhyme, pray tell?” Sister Maggie asked.

“ ‘Ten Little Monkeys Jumping on the Bed.’ ”

Sister Maggie nodded. “The other day, I heard the little ones at our parish daycare singing that song. They ended up in a fit of giggles before the song was finished.”

“As a matter of fact, Leo rolls over on his side and can’t stop laughing when I serenade him.”

“Do any of you ever go into his habitat?” Sister Maggie asked.

Souter responded. “Zoo policy prohibits zookeepers and visitors from interacting with orangutans within their enclosures. Only Sam is exempted from the policy since they’ve had a relationship nearly all of Leo’s life.”

Sister Maggie turned to Sam. “Really, how fascinating. How long have you worked with Leo?”

“I was living in Borneo at the time, when a poacher shot Leo’s mother,” Sam said. “Fortunately, Leo’s mother lived long enough to hide among some bushes. She died holding Leo in a protective embrace,” he said, his voice cracking, his eyes downcast. “Another conservationist and I helped rescue Leo. Sorry, I still get choked up when I talk about it.”

“How tragic,” Sister Maggie said as she observed Sam’s emotional reaction. It was understandable that Sam was emotional. But she saw something more to his reaction. Something in his eyes. His gaze had skittered away.

“But you saved Leo, and that is a blessing, don’t you agree?”

“Yes, yes, of course, it is.” Sam cleared his throat. “I worked at the New York State Zoo and helped hand-raise him with two other zookeepers.

“When Leo came here, I applied for a transfer. Luckily, Dr. Souter decided to hire me for my current position. I’ve been here a few months,” Sam said.

Sister Maggie couldn't quite put her finger on it, but the more she studied Sam's eyes, the more she sensed he carried a heavy burden. Was it related to the loss of Leo's mother, perhaps? The poachers? Leo having been orphaned? No, the young man was definitely troubled about something that had happened far more recently than Leo's rescue.

"It's such a tragedy that these amazing creatures are hunted down," Sister Mary Felicia said.

"It is a tragedy," Bob agreed. "They're hunted for their meat, while the babies are sold on the black market as pets for outrageous sums to people who have no idea what they're doing, other than they want an exotic pet."

Sister Maggie shook her head. "There are so many domesticated animals like cats and dogs who need good homes. Why people feel the need to keep exotic pets is nothing but an extreme kind of selfishness. They certainly don't think about what's best for the wild animal."

"Good point, Sister Maggie," Sister Mary Felicia said.

"Thank you. Sometimes I do make a good point or two." Sister Maggie smiled. She pulled out a wide-brimmed white hat from her cloth shopping bag and placed it on her head to shield her face from the sun. Leo immediately moved closer to her and sat down. He stared at her hat and pointed to it.

"Leo likes your hat, Sister Maggie," Jaime said.

"I do believe you're right." Sister Maggie smiled again as Leo came even closer to the fence.

"Hats, jewelry, tattoos, and cell phones fascinate Leo," said Charlie. "Anything that looks like an adornment."

Leo again pointed to Sister Maggie's hat.

"He wants you to take it off so he can look at it," Sam said. "He's a curious fellow."

"Well, I can relate to that." Sister Maggie removed her hat and brought it up to the fence. She turned it around slowly several times. Leo seemed to lose interest in the hat after the third rotation. Then he pointed with his index finger at the silver crucifix around her neck.

Sister Maggie lifted it, kissed it, and gave Leo a close-up view of the religious symbol. He stared intently at it for a few moments then he moved to where Sister Mary Felicia stood. He stared at her and gestured with his hands.

"What's he saying?" Sister Mary Felicia asked.

"He's requesting the monkey song," Sam said as he began gesturing. "Not now, Leo. Later on, maybe." Leo made an exaggerated face and turned his back on the group as though pouting.

He's like a child, Sister Maggie thought.

"He'll get over it," Bob said. "He's a smart-aleck for sure."

They all had a good laugh at that.

"How did he get the name Leo?" Sister Maggie asked.

"After I introduced him to edible finger paints and taught him to use a canvas, he turned into a major show-off," Sam said. "So I started calling him Leo after Leonardo da Vinci. If anyone is watching, he'll raise his brush, dip it in the paint, lick off some of the paint, then smear the rest on the canvas. He watches how visitors react, and if someone makes a comment, he'll make even more dramatic strokes. Leo took to his new name very quickly."

Leo turned back to face his audience. Sister Maggie noted he was no longer making the pouting face. Leo put his index finger through the fence and waited for Sam to extend his own index finger so that the tips of their fingers touched.

"He's apologizing for his little tantrum," said Sam.

Sister Maggie looked at the scene with amazement. The image of their index fingers touching reminded her of Michelangelo's fresco of God giving life to the first man, Adam.

Leo retracted his finger and focused his attention on Bob Souter. As though remembering their encounter that morning, he signed something. Sam and Charlie looked at each other and turned away from each other to keep from laughing.

"He can be naughty, like a toddler," remarked Charlie.

"What did he sign to you, Sam?" Sister Mary Felicia asked.

"Stink Man, go away. Leo mad."

Everyone laughed. "Has Leo ever been tested to determine his level of intelligence as compared to a human child?" Sister Maggie asked.

"Through a number of cognitive tests, Leo scored at the level of a two-year-old," Sam replied. "If that's not impressive enough, Leo's freestyle drawings resemble those of a three-year-old."

Sam was interrupted by a call on his walkie-talkie. "I'll be there in a few minutes." He turned to Sisters Maggie and Mary Felicia, "Sisters, I'll have to excuse myself. One of our female orangutans developed a severe bacterial infection. I have to supervise the cleaning crew as they wash down her enclosure," Sam added.

"I'll go with you, Sam," Charlie offered. "It's been a pleasure to meet y'all," Charlie said as she waved good-bye.

"It was a great pleasure to meet you as well, Charlie," Sister Maggie said.

Sam turned to Leo, who'd been watching them with what Sister Maggie surmised as a curious expression from the other side of the fence.

"Be good, Leo. See you later," Sam gestured to the orangutan.

Leo gestured back and then pointed at Sisters Maggie and Mary Felicia.

"Leo says good-bye to you both," Sam laughed.

"I'll come back another time to sing to you," Sister Mary Felicia said.

Leo cocked his head and waved his huge hand.

Sisters Maggie and Mary Felicia waved back.

"Hope to see you at the fundraising dinner tomorrow night," Charlie said over her shoulder as she trailed behind Sam.

"Fundraising dinner?" Sister Maggie turned to Sister Mary Felicia, who shrugged.

"We would love to invite you both to our annual fundraising dinner tomorrow night. It's always a fun event, and I promise you'll have a wonderful time," Bob said with a smile.

"Well, in that case, how can we say no?" Sister Maggie grinned. "What do you say, Sister Mary Felicia?"

"I can't wait."

"Terrific. Let's continue our tour of the zoo," Jaime suggested.

"Sounds like a plan," Sister Maggie said. "Although I'd love to come back one day and learn a few signs and have another chat with Leo."

"I'm sure we can arrange that," Bob said.

"Where to next, Jaime?" Sister Mary Felicia asked.

"Our next destination is the Wildlife of Africa exhibit."

Bob Souter called out, "All aboard."

CHAPTER THREE

April 16, 12:30 p.m.
Indiana State Zoo
Indianapolis, Indiana

"WHAT A FUN TOUR," Sister Maggie said to Bob and Jaime. "Could you fellows drop me off at the nearest public restroom? I'll meet you all at the café shortly."

"We can certainly wait for you," Jaime offered.

"No. You three young people go on. I won't be long. Order me an iced tea, Sister Mary Felicia."

"Will do, Sister Maggie."

Sister Maggie stepped down from the cart and walked briskly to the restrooms. Once inside, she gasped and froze in place and couldn't help but stare at the six stalls painted green. A shiver traveled up her spine. She would never forget the image in her mind of the green bathroom stalls at the Florida amusement park where Catie disappeared. It had been emblazoned in her mind for decades. She stepped inside one of the stalls and tried to shake off the feeling that something wasn't right.

Flushing the toilet, she opened the stall door and gasped when she saw a young girl of about thirteen with shoulder-length red hair standing by the sinks.

Catie!

Her twin sister wore the same navy shorts and blue-and-white striped tank top she had on when she disappeared all those years ago. She was holding a stuffed bear with glass-blue eyes that she'd won in the coin toss game.

"Catie!" Tears streamed down Sister Maggie's face. "What are you trying to tell me, Red?" Red had been Catie's nickname when they were children. Even though they were identical twins and both had bright red hair, Catie was called Red, and Sister Maggie was called Clancy or "red warrior" because she was prone to getting into fights, usually while standing up to a bully.

Maggie and Catie were the eldest, with four younger brothers—John Jr. who they all called Johnny, Matt, and Dennis, had all gone into law enforcement like her late beloved father, John Sr., while the youngest brother, Andrew, had become a priest. They all still lived in New York and visited their mother, Lulu, who was still stirring up trouble in a seniors' apartment complex.

Sister Maggie adored her family and visited them as often as she could. And although they had shared many great memories through the years, the dark specter of Catie's disappearance still hung over them. A cold case, it was called. Last year, when she was in New York visiting her family, Sister Maggie had had several psychic experiences while helping her goddaughter Ellie cope with a husband who turned out to be a killer and a sociopath. Thanks to Sister Maggie's psychic skills, along with help from Ellie's former fiancé, David, they stopped Ellie's husband and his mentally unstable brother from committing more atrocities.

It was also back in New York that Sister Maggie experienced unsettling visions of Catie through visions of the day Catie disappeared.

Sister Maggie held her breath, wanting so much to take a step toward Catie, but her feet remained fixed to the floor as though glued.

Catie shook her head as though reminding Sister Maggie that it was not possible for them to embrace or hold each other again in this life. Between them lay a chasm that could be crossed only through death.

"Catie..." Sister Maggie swallowed the lump in her throat. "Last time I saw you—you showed me a young man wearing a white T-shirt, jeans, and a black baseball cap. And his t-shirt had the word COACH on the back. Can you show me something more about him? Can you tell me anything more? Where did he take you, Catie?"

Catie put her stuffed animal down and turned toward the sink. She pointed to the commercial liquid soap dispenser affixed to the wall.

Again, Sister Maggie felt another surge through her body like an electrical current. This time, she heard someone knocking on her stall door.

"Ma'am, are you all right?" a voice called out.

Sister Maggie's eyes widened as she realized she'd never left the bathroom stall. She took a tissue from her pocket and wiped tears from her eyes.

"I'm fine," Sister Maggie called back. Taking a deep breath, she opened the stall door and saw two women staring at her, one holding a baby.

"We heard you cry out to someone named Catie," the older woman said as Sister Maggie walked toward the sink.

"I apologize to all of you," Sister Maggie said with a smile. "She removed her cell phone from her blue tunic pocket. I was talking to someone. It's a long story...I'm so sorry I alarmed you."

"Bad news?" the younger woman holding the baby asked.

Sister Maggie nodded. "Thank you all for your concern. I'll be fine."

"Well, we're just relieved you're okay," the older woman replied.

"Yes, thank you. I am." Sister Maggie smiled over her shoulder. She pumped the soap dispenser and watched as the pink-colored industrial liquid soap oozed into her hands. For a moment, she stared at it.

Catie, what were you trying to show me?

She turned on the faucet and lathered and rinsed her hands. Her gaze landed on the name of the company imprinted on the front of the dispenser. Plucking a paper towel from the dispenser, she dried her hands and then lifted her black-framed glasses to the bifocal area and read ARS INDUSTRIAL CLEANING SUPPLIES.

Could ARS be the initials of the killer? Or is that too easy? I'll have to think more about this later when I have time.

Taking her purse, she exited the bathroom and headed to the café, all the while pondering the vision of Catie and the letters ARS.

CHAPTER FOUR

April 17, 6:30 p.m.
Dolphin Pavilion at Indiana State Zoo
Indianapolis, Indiana

THE SMILING dolphin was so close, Sister Maggie reached out and touched it. "What a lovely paper lantern."

"Yes, they were made for this event by a local artist, Joanna D'Angelo," Jaime said. "Joanna is super-talented. She couldn't make it tonight, but she donated all these marine and animal wildlife fixtures for the evening. We'll be raffling them off later as part of the prizes."

"How delightful." Sister Maggie spotted a panda bear hanging over the next table, a giraffe across the aisle, and behind them a lovely zebra. "She *is* super-talented," Sister Maggie quipped, using Jaime's expression. "I'd love to see more of her work."

"You're in luck," Jaime said. "Joanna will be holding an exhibition in September to help raise funds for the new wing of the children's hospital."

"What a wonderful idea," Sister Maggie said. "I would definitely like to be involved in that."

"I'm sure she'll need volunteers," Sister Mary Felicia said. "I'll look into it. Perhaps we can make it a community work project for the kids at the parish."

Sister Maggie nodded her approval. One of their goals for the children and teens in the parish, especially those who came from prominent and financially well-off families, was to encourage them to be active in community service. Sister Maggie had established a volunteer youth program in the parish. Volunteerism was something Sister Maggie firmly believed in, thanks to Lulu, who had instilled in Sister Maggie and her brothers that success in life started by learning the value of sacrifice through service. Lulu insisted that only by serving others could they discover their own true potential.

Sister Maggie's thoughts were interrupted as servers entered the dining room carrying large serving platters. "Is the entire meal vegan?"

"Yes, compliments of the Vegans for Life Organization," Jaime replied.

"And don't forget gluten-free, peanut-free, egg-and dairy-free," Sister Mary Felicia chirped.

Sister Maggie noted Sister Mary Felicia's mouth had quirked suspiciously with what she surmised as someone trying very hard not to giggle.

"Well, I am certainly open to new culinary adventures," Sister Maggie declared as a young woman placed salads in front of them.

"I think you'll find the meal quite tasty," Charlie replied.

Sister Maggie smiled at the young woman who looked stunning in a simple black dress, her black hair wrapped into a sleek topknot. They were seated at a round table in the middle section of the banquet hall. Another zookeeper named Juan Espinoza sat with Jaime, Sister Mary Felicia, and Charlie.

Sister Maggie tucked into her colorful salad, enjoying the mix of artichokes, cherry tomatoes, spring onions, and crisp English cucumber drizzled with lemon juice and extra virgin olive oil. A large basket of gluten-free breadsticks baked with rosemary and garlic sat in the center of the table. Sister Maggie had dipped one into the olive oil dressing and took a bite, savoring the melding of flavors and the satisfying crunch of the toasted bread.

So far, so good. I might have to go vegan more often.

"I'm surprised Sam isn't here yet. He's always so punctual," Jaime noted with a glance at his wristwatch. Jaime picked up his cell phone and called Sam. "It's gone to voicemail. This is so unlike him. We've been friends since college. You can set your clock by him."

"Maybe's he on a Burger Heaven run for Leo." Sister Mary Felicia winked at her cousin.

"He told me he wanted to check on Leo before he came over," Charlie whispered. "He actually was going to sneak him half a Stack Five Burger."

"Against Dr. Souter's orders?" Jaime asked.

"Sam doesn't give Leo unhealthy food very often. Even my husband, Dale, who's a vet, says an occasional treat won't hurt Leo," Charlie said in a defensive tone.

"Is your husband a vet at the Indiana State Zoo?" asked Sister Maggie, trying to change the subject.

"No. He owns the Woodbury Animal Clinic in Indianapolis. I help him on Saturdays," Charlie replied.

"Speaking of Sam," Juan chimed in. "Did you know he was a criminal prosecutor in New York before he started hanging out with apes?"

"I had no idea," Sister Maggie said before crunching into another bite.

"He doesn't talk about it much," Juan added. "He mentioned once he prosecuted a case against a white supremacy group, and the case went wrong. He had to recuse himself for some reason and wanted to get as far away as he could. So he ended up in Borneo."

"Lucky for us, that's where he became involved in the conservation movement," Charlie said with a slight frown at Juan.

"Something bad led to something good," Sister Maggie added.

"I guess you can look at it that way," Juan said. "Speaking of bad to good—I'm going to search for some protein, even if I have to steal peanut butter crackers from a vending machine." With a grin, he stood and excused himself.

"Well, I guess the vegan meal didn't go over well with Juan," Sister Mary Felicia said with a grin. "How are you coping, Sister Maggie?"

"I'll stick it out. Besides, Burger Heaven is on the way home just in case." She winked.

As they were finishing up the main course—roasted red-pepper gnocchi with a vegan tomato sauce, Sister Maggie spied a former parishioner, Barry Pryce, heading for their table in an agitated state. The stout CPA was an avid conservationist, and a year ago, he'd accepted a job in Indianapolis and had begun to attend another Catholic Church closer to his new home.

Barry was wheezing slightly as he reached their table. He whispered something in Jaime's ear, then pulled out his inhaler and took a deep puff.

Sister Maggie, heard a few whispered words: "...just lying there."

"My apologies, everyone," Jaime announced. "But I need to excuse myself to take care of some zoo business. Please enjoy your meal," he urged as he stood and turned to leave.

Sister Maggie watched Jaime dash for the exit, followed by a huffing and puffing Bryce.

"Something is terribly wrong," Sister Mary Felicia whispered. "Jaime's face was as white as a sheet."

Sister Maggie heard the distinct drone of sirens just as Sister Mary Felicia urged her to find out what was happening.

"Why don't we go check things out? Do you want to come with me?" Sister Maggie asked.

"I think Jaime would scold me for chasing after him like a mother hen," Sister Mary Felicia said.

A few minutes later, as the lights were dimmed for a presentation on deforestation in Borneo and Sumatra that directly affected the orangutan populations in Southeast Asia, Sister Maggie made her escape from the Dolphin Pavilion. She headed toward the flashing lights near the orangutan enclosure. She stood behind an overgrown bush and parted some of the branches to get a better look.

She gasped at what she saw. There, lying face down next to a very agitated Leo on the other side of the fence, was a motionless Sam.

God rest his soul. Sister Maggie said a silent prayer for the young man.

"...shot execution-style. One bullet between his eyes," one of the officers stated to Jaime, who looked as shocked as Sister Maggie felt. Jaime's hands covered his mouth as he looked away from Sam's lifeless body.

This is no random act of violence or a crime gone wrong, Sister Maggie thought. Whoever had killed Sam execution-style must have known exactly what he or she was doing. Sister Maggie's mind whirled. Sam had told them yesterday about Leo's mother being the victim of poachers, but that was in Borneo. In the U.S., thieves and marauders of a different kind targeted the human population. Maybe Sam's murderer was a former inmate—someone Sam had put behind bars during the time he'd worked as a prosecutor? Or a cohort or family member of an inmate wanting to even the score?

Leo started pulling on the enclosure's fence as though trying to pry it open. A moment later, he collected several rocks and ran up the ladder that had him overlooking the outside station over Sam's body, the police, Jaime, and Barry. Leo began throwing the rocks at the police officers who'd draped Sam's body with a white sheet.

"Tell that ape to cut it out!" shouted one of the officers after a rock hit him on the shoulder. Jaime picked up his walkie-talkie and called for one of the zookeepers to coax Leo inside.

Sister Maggie swallowed the lump in her throat as she witnessed Leo's grief, for that was the only way she could attribute a meaning to Leo's actions. She could not see Leo's face clearly from where she was, even though it was still light out. But she could tell by the very act of throwing the rocks at the officers and by his flailing arms that he was distraught.

Poor Leo.

Sister Maggie knew her presence at the crime scene would not be appreciated. Besides, she had to get back to Sister Mary Felicia and tell her the dreadful news. She turned around and made her way back to the Dolphin Pavilion with a heavy heart.

CHAPTER FIVE

April 17, 10:30 p.m.
Our Lady of Guadalupe Convent
New Hope, Indiana

"IT'S SHOCKING. TRULY SHOCKING."

Sister Maggie nodded at Sister Mary Felicia's statement as she pulled into the winding drive of the convent. "Yes. It is shocking."

"I mean, who would want to kill Sam?" Sister Mary Felicia continued. "He was such a nice guy and so devoted to Leo and the other animals at the zoo."

"Murder has no meaning. It's senseless and destructive."

"I wonder if the police found anything significant at the crime scene?"

"Well, I'm sure the crime scene investigators will find something. The two officers who responded to the call aren't detectives. They would have called in for support." Sister Maggie had filled in Sister Mary Felicia about everything she'd observed from her vantage point behind the bushes, including Leo's aggressive rock-throwing behavior.

"Poor Leo. He must be heartbroken. When you saw him hurling

stones at the police, it was as though he was trying to make them stop. He didn't want anyone to touch his beloved friend's body," said Sister Mary Felicia as she shook her head.

"Perhaps it was his way of expressing grief. I would like to find out more about that, though," Sister Maggie said as they got out of the car.

"Why?" Sister Felicia asked.

"Because I believe Leo was a witness to the murder."

"You're kidding."

"No, and I'd like to learn more about Sam and Leo's mode of communications."

"Maybe Jaime would be open to that as well. He was so shaken when he came back to tell Bob and Charlie," Sister Mary Felicia said as she slipped her key into the lock of the front door. Suddenly the door flew open to reveal a wide-eyed Sister Ruthie.

"Thank goodness you're both home."

"What's wrong?" Sister Maggie asked.

"The convent is haunted!" Sister Rose Marie exclaimed, rushing up to the entry hall just as Sister Ruthie had opened her mouth to speak.

"Haunted?" Sister Mary Felicia asked.

Sister Mary Frances joined them. "Strange things started happening this evening while you were at that banquet dinner."

"Hm…stranger things still," Sister Maggie mumbled. "Why don't we all go into the kitchen for a cup of hot chocolate, and you can fill us in on these strange things."

"Hot chocolate?" Sister Ruthie piped up. "We're in the middle of a heat wave."

"Well, you can drink yours cold," Sister Maggie said with a smile.

A few minutes later, the sisters sat around the kitchen table drinking hot chocolate or cold beverages.

"Now, you mentioned multiple strange things. Tell me everything you witnessed tonight, and we'll figure out what happened."

It wasn't that Sister Maggie didn't believe in the existence of the supernatural. Far from it. After all, as a young nun, she'd assisted the good priest, Father Timothy O'Connor, in an exorcism as a prayer participant. It was then she realized being at the side of an exorcist—

even performing the simple ministry of prayer—was too much for her.

Furthermore, she was too often the recipient of dreams and visions from those who'd passed on. She recalled the vision she had in the public restroom at the zoo only yesterday, not to mention the dreams about Marcy Holmes's murder last year.

At least those visions of Marcy had enabled Sister Maggie to help her goddaughter, Ellie, during that frightening time when her husband had been threatening her. Sister Maggie's visions of Catie had, so far, only yielded a few clues as to her disappearance and murder more than fifty years ago. But she was ever hopeful Catie would reach out once more, somehow, and communicate additional information to help her learn the identity of the person who had kidnapped and killed her.

Sister Maggie wondered about the name of the company imprinted on the soap dispenser in the restroom of the Indiana State Zoo. *ARS INDUSTRIAL CLEANING SUPPLIES.* She sipped her hot chocolate and sighed. She would need to research the company, but at the moment, she had to figure out what was going on at the convent.

"It happened earlier this evening while we were having dinner," Sister Mary Frances began.

Sister Ruthie piped up. "As we were enjoying our light meal of pears and cheese with that delicious French baguette we purchased at Le Moulin Rouge Bakery on Davenport Road—by the way, we purchased two more and put them in the freez—"

"Sister Ruthie, you can tell them about the food later," Sister Rose Marie interrupted.

"Yes, my apologies," Sister Ruthie said, fingering the beads of her blue rosary. "I told the sisters about my odd experience. Then, Sister Rose Marie and Sister Mary Frances both said they each had had a strange experience today as well." Sister Ruthie hesitated.

"Go on, dear Sister Ruthie," Sister Maggie said in encouragement. "If we are to solve this mystery, then we must know the facts. Tell me what you each experienced first, and then we shall unravel this."

Sister Ruthie gathered her rosary and cupped it in the palm of her hand. “I was in the front office answering the telephone. Suddenly, I heard the television blasting in the community room. When I hung up the phone, I went into the room and found no one there, and strangely, the remote was on the floor and not where we usually keep it, on the TV stand.”

“And Sister Rose Marie, tell us about your experience,” Sister Maggie said.

“I was in the kitchen cleaning out the refrigerator when I was startled by a loud crash coming from the laundry room. When I went in to look, the soap powder on the top shelf had fallen to the ground but not before it knocked down two of the tabletop drying racks.”

“Now, Sister Mary Frances, please share what happened to you,” Sister Maggie requested.

“While I was taking a shower this morning, I heard the 4-tier metal bathroom tower with all our towels and accessories topple over. I nearly had a heart attack. I wrapped a towel around myself and opened the shower door only to realize I was quite alone, but the bathroom door was wide open.”

“If those occurrences had happened on separate days, I would not think them so odd, but they happened all in the same day, so that gives us pause, doesn’t it?” Sister Maggie said.

The women all nodded in agreement as they sipped their drinks.

The sound of weeping floated into the kitchen.

“Oh, my goodness,” Sister Rose Marie whispered. “Did you hear that?”

“It sounds like a baby crying,” Sister Ruthie said in alarm.

“You see,” Sister Mary Frances declared. “We were not exaggerating. This convent is haunted, I tell you. We must contact the exorcist at once.”

“Hush,” Sister Maggie said, holding her index finger to her mouth. She got up from the table and did a slow turn of the room to try to determine where the mournful crying was coming from.

“Uh-oh,” Sister Mary Felicia whispered.

Sister Maggie turned to the young woman and noticed her face was red and flushed. She wondered why the young nun looked embarrassed and then it clicked into place. Sister Maggie crossed her arms over her chest and regarded Sister Mary Felicia with raised brows. "Spill the beans."

"Um—okay, I need to apologize for not telling you all sooner. What with everything going on at the zoo—" her voice petered out and then she took a deep breath. "A couple of days ago, I was in the rectory garage searching for the bicycle pump. The tires on my bike were getting a little deflated, and I needed to get them in ship-shape for the annual parish bike race."

"Stick to the pertinent facts," Sister Maggie interrupted, knowing Sister Mary Felicia was stalling.

"Well, you see, I heard crying that sounded like a baby, coming from just outside the side door of the garage. So, I went to investigate. I opened the door, and there was a mewling ball of fur behind that big old, cracked flowerpot."

"A baby?" Sister Ruthie exclaimed, her hand on her chest.

"Babies don't have fur," Sister Rose Marie said.

"No, a kitten. The cutest, little black kitten. She was all alone—I have no idea how she got there. Perhaps she'd been abandoned by her mother, or she'd just lost her way. In any case, I brought her inside. She looked to be about six weeks old and quite thin. It was so hot, I didn't think she'd survive if I didn't act fast. I set up a little box in my bedroom with a towel, then I gave her some water and bites of tuna. And when she'd fallen asleep, I went out to get some supplies. She's a bit mischievous, but she's a good kitten. So very sweet."

"I was wondering why you've kept your bedroom door shut for the past few days," Sister Mary Frances said.

"The problem with my door is that it doesn't stay shut. I bet that's how the kitten escaped."

"I think we have discovered the truth behind those strange occurrences, haven't we sisters?" Sister Maggie asked with raised eyebrows.

They all started laughing as they realized the rambunctious kitten had certainly made its presence known.

"I'm very sorry I didn't tell you all. The truth is, I was trying to figure out what to do next," Sister Mary Felicia said. "I was hoping… maybe, we could keep her?"

The older nuns exchanged glances and then nodded in agreement, their eyes twinkling with mirth.

"Well, now that we have decided to keep the little rascal, where is she?" Sister Maggie asked.

Sister Mary Felicia began to make kissing sounds. Suddenly, a little black ball of fur scampered in from the hallway and jumped up on Sister Mary Felicia's lap. She lifted the kitten to her chest and cuddled it. Then she passed it around for the other nuns to hold. Sister Maggie smiled as she tickled the kitten behind its ears. "What an adorable little mite."

"I do apologize to all of you for keeping you in the dark about the kitten. With Sam Browning's murder earlier tonight, it slipped my mind." Sister Mary Felicia took the kitten back and hugged it to her chest.

The sisters gasped in shock when they learned about the murder and started firing questions out left, right, and center.

Sister Maggie calmed them down and filled them in on the tragic events during the charity dinner. Sister Ruthie got up and took the tin of cookies from the pantry cupboard.

"This calls for at least a vanilla cream and maybe a chocolate chip," she declared as she lifted the lid and offered the sisters each a cookie.

"I wish all life's mysteries were as easy to solve as this one," Sister Maggie said as she patted the kitten's head. "Well, we have to give this precious creature a name. Any suggestions?"

Again, Sister Mary Felicia's face reddened. "I started to call her Courtney. It was my favorite name for one of my dolls when I was a little girl."

"I adore that name," Sister Mary Frances said, reaching for her second cookie.

The other nuns agreed.

"Well, Courtney it shall be." Sister Maggie said, plucking a cookie from the tin. She was glad they could all enjoy the kitten's antics. They certainly needed it after the tragedy of Sam Browning's murder.

CHAPTER SIX

April 18, 2:00 a.m.
Our Lady of Guadalupe Convent
New Hope, Indiana

"COURTNEY, IS THAT YOU?" Sister Maggie whispered at the sound of scratching on her bedroom door. She glanced at the clock. It was two in the morning. She got up and opened the door, and the tiny black kitten scurried in and leaped onto Sister Maggie's bed.

"Why aren't you fast asleep in the lovely little bed Sister Mary Felicia set up in her room?" Sister Maggie said, hands on hips.

The hallway nightlight illuminated Courtney, who had paused to lick her paw. She stopped and looked up to regard Sister Maggie with placid green eyes.

"So, what's your plan for tonight?" asked Sister Maggie. She sat on the side of the bed, picked up the kitten, and cuddled her against her chest. "You're a little troublemaker. You had the sisters thinking this place was haunted."

The kitten rubbed her face against Sister Maggie's shoulder. That's when the serious purring began. "You're quite the operator, aren't you?" Sister Maggie whispered as she placed Courtney at the foot of her bed. "Time to go to sleep, little runt." She rubbed the kitten's head until the kitten closed her eyes and fell asleep.

"Good kitty," she said as she quietly slid back in bed so as not to wake Courtney. She adjusted her pillow and closed her eyes. She was exhausted, shocked, and saddened by what had happened at the zoo. Her last thoughts focused on Sam Browning as he lay motionless on the ground with a bullet in his head. Her eyelids began to get heavy, and she found herself drifting off once more.

Sister Maggie's eyes flew open. Something had woken her up. She looked down by her feet and saw the kitten fast asleep. There it was. A sound coming from down the hall. Glancing at the clock, she noticed it was just after three in the morning. She rose from the bed, took her robe from the chair, slipped it on, and slid her feet into her slippers. She glanced into the hallway and noticed it was in complete darkness. She figured the hallway nightlight had probably burned out.

She stepped back into her room and retrieved the flashlight she kept in the drawer of her bedside table. She returned to the corridor and pointed the beam of light as she made her way down the second-floor hallway. The unusual sound got louder, reminding her of a running stream. The sound was coming from the guest bedroom. She turned the doorknob and stepped inside. Holding her flashlight, she did a slow turn in the room. Her eyes widened at what she saw...

Stainless steel cabinets ran along one wall with a double stainless steel sink. A long metal table sat in the center of the room. She walked farther into the room and spied an array of medical equipment in the corner. *An operating room? Or some kind of lab?*

Sister Maggie's eyes narrowed as she felt a presence behind her. She instinctively knew it was a human spirit. She turned and held her flashlight high, realizing the long metal table was no longer bare. It was now covered with a white sheet, and something, or rather someone, lay beneath it. Her heartbeat kicked into high gear as she saw a movement beneath the sheet. She gasped as an arm emerged and pulled the sheet away. She watched the sheet fall to the ground. Sam Browning's body was now visible.

Calm down, Clancy.

The zookeeper turned his face in her direction. That's when she saw the hole in his forehead.

"I'm so sorry you were murdered, Sam," Sister Maggie said. No matter how many times the dead came to her in dreams and visions, she always felt humbled. She didn't know why she had this ability to communicate with people after they passed, but she was thankful for it. Thankful and humbled. Although some of her visions shook her to the core, she didn't fear those who reached out to her. Most times, they were trying to get an important message to a loved one. No, it was the living she feared. Those who did evil in the world chilled her bones.

"Sam, why am I here? What do you want to tell me?"

Suddenly, Sam's body heaved up and then collapsed back on the table with a thud. A metallic clang resounded as something fell onto the cold tile floor. Sister Maggie's flashlight followed an object that rolled in her direction. It was a bullet. It stopped at her feet, and she bent down to pick it up. She held it in the palm of her hand and focused her flashlight on it as she examined it. A moment later, it was gone. Vanished.

Some force began to pull her away from the lab. Everything began to fade from view. Her flashlight flickered off, and she stumbled back. She reached out to grasp onto something to break her fall, but there was nothing...She gasped and her eyes flew open. She felt something soft beneath her and realized she was back in her bed. She gripped the sheets as though they were an anchor. She took a deep breath to steady herself and felt an unusual weight on her chest. Opening her eyes, she saw the little ball of black fur curled up on her chest. Courtney stared back at her, her head tilted, her gaze curious. The sight of the kitten made Sister Maggie smile, and oddly, made her feel safe. She rubbed Courtney's back, and the kitten purred in response.

"Sweetie, you have to sleep at the foot of the bed," she whispered. "We need a serious understanding about personal space." She gently lifted the kitten and once again placed her at the end of the bed. Courtney again curled up in a ball and was no worse for the move.

Sister Maggie sat up and turned on her lamp. She opened the

drawer to her night table. She took out her journal and began to document what she'd seen in her dream. She'd begun to keep a journal after Catie died. Her school guidance counselor at the time, Mrs. Hawkins, gave her a journal with red leather binding and suggested she write her thoughts down, that it would help. It did. From that point on, she'd kept a journal. She'd filled many pages over the years, and always in a journal with red leather binding. She didn't know why she always bought the same type. Perhaps it was the feeling it evoked —a connection to Mrs. Hawkins who had always been so kind. Sister Maggie closed her eyes and pictured the bullet in the palm of her hand. She opened her eyes and sketched it as best she could.

As a New York City police captain, her father, John Senior, had introduced Clancy to the use of firearms when she was a teenager. By the time Clancy turned eighteen, she could hit targets like a pro. John Senior had also taught young Clancy about the different makes of guns and ammunition. At one time, Clancy had wanted to follow in her father's footsteps and join the police force. Her father was dead set against it. Eventually, she let go of that dream when she'd recognized her true calling to become a sister. But even though John Sr. had been opposed to Clancy becoming a police officer, along with her younger brothers, he had taken the time to teach them all. Clancy's mother, Lulu, believed it was because of Catie. Their father wanted them to be able to protect themselves. Knowledge was power.

Sister Maggie stared at her sketch of the bullet. "Clancy, this is a very unusual bullet," John Sr. would have said. "Won't fit a modern gun, that's for sure."

Yes, Dad, you're right. A very unusual bullet, indeed.

CHAPTER SEVEN

April 18, 8:30 a.m.
Our Lady of Guadalupe Convent
New Hope, Indiana

"Sister Mary Felicia, your cousin is on line one," Sister Rose Marie said, putting the call on hold.

"Thanks, Sister Rose Marie. I'll take the call in the front office." Sister Mary Felicia got up from the kitchen table and headed down the hall.

Sister Maggie hoped it wasn't more bad news. She took a sip of her coffee, then set it back down and resumed her research on her tablet.

"What on earth are you looking at?" asked Sister Ruthie.

"Bullets. I'm looking at bullets," Sister Maggie said without looking up.

"Why are you looking at bullets?" prodded Sister Ruthie. "Did something inspire you during our meditation this morning in the chapel?"

Sister Maggie smiled. "Just doing some research."

"I hope you're not planning to buy a gun and shoot Bishop Boyle. I know you were upset with his decision to move your brother, Father

Andrew, out of Queens to some godforsaken place in Brooklyn. What was the reason, anyway?"

Sister Maggie regarded Sister Ruthie over the rim of her glasses. The older nun was known for her bluntness. "Andrew believes the church should provide greater accountability to the parishioners, financially and otherwise."

"I heard talk about Bishop Boyle and a gun," Sister Mary Frances said as she joined them at the table. "Should we be worried?"

"Sister Maggie is researching guns and bullets," Sister Ruthie said. "I asked if she were thinking of shooting Bishop Boyle after he transferred our lovable Beach Boy, Andrew, to another parish."

"Oh, I wouldn't shoot the bishop," Sister Maggie quipped without missing a beat. "I'd ask one of my brothers. They're all great marksmen."

Sister Rose Marie put her hands on her hips. "Always the jokester. Seriously, how is Andy doing these days?"

Sister Maggie smiled. "Our loveable Beach Boy, as Sister Ruthie calls him, has abundant faith—"

"Along with an abundant collection of Hawaiian shirts," Sister Ruthie interrupted.

The sisters giggled at that.

"Too true, but he's fine with the transfer. Andy says no matter why he was told to leave St. Gabriel's by the bishop, God would bless his ministry among the people he'd be sent to serve. And that's true. Even for us. In obedience, we go forth to accomplish not our will, but God's."

Sister Mary Felicia returned to the kitchen. "Sister Maggie, since we're driving into Indianapolis this morning to check out the booths for the fair, would you mind if we took a side trip to the Indiana State Zoo?"

Sister Maggie cocked her head to one side. "Does this have anything to do with Leo?"

Sister Mary Felicia nodded. "Jaime said the team is worried about Leo because of Sam's death. He suggested we stop by for a visit, and I can sing to him. It may help calm him down."

"Well, if we leave in the next few minutes, we can spend some time at the zoo and then get to the fairgrounds in plenty of time to talk to Mr. Corbett about booth rentals and locations," Sister Maggie said. "I'm determined to avoid being downwind from the prize hogs this year."

"Earl, Merle, and Pearl were so darling," Sister Rose Marie said.

"Certainly, if your sole purpose is to visit the pigs. I'd rather secure a booth close to the food carts so we can attract more young people."

Sister Mary Felicia's eyes widened at the images of the bullets on Sister Maggie's tablet. "Why are you looking at bullets?"

"She's ordering bullets," Sister Ruthie said as she loaded up the dishwasher. "She's going to shoot Bishop Boyle."

Sister Mary Felicia gasped. "What?"

Sisters Mary Frances and Rose Marie began to laugh.

"Very funny. This is how rumors start," Sister Maggie said. "Besides, you got it wrong. I said I would get one of my brothers to shoot him."

CHAPTER EIGHT

April 18, 10:00 a.m.
The Indiana State Zoo
Indianapolis, Indiana

"THANKS FOR COMING TODAY," Jaime said. "Charlie will meet us at the enclosure where Leo has been for the last couple of hours. He won't budge. It's like he's waiting for Sam to stroll up and sign to him."

"Have you tried giving him one of those burgers he loves?" Sister Mary Felicia asked. "Maybe it will offer him some comfort."

Jaime patted a blue pouch he had dangling from his shoulder. "It's right here. Don't mention it to Dr. Souter. He certainly doesn't want Leo to get hooked on junk food as a way to comfort himself. Then again, if Leo refuses the burger, I don't know what we'll do. The one constant in Leo's life from infancy was Sam. Leo may understand that something terrible happened to Sam and he won't be back."

"From what I've been told, Leo understands the concept of death," remarked Sister Maggie.

Jaime nodded in agreement "When he sees dead zoo animals being carted away and covered over, he signs to us that they are draped. Draped means death in his mind."

Sister Maggie nodded. "He probably saw Sam's body covered or draped with a sheet when his body was removed from the crime scene."

"Leo watched everything, including when the police and the paramedics arrived and loaded Sam's body into the ambulance," Jaime said as he assisted Sister Maggie and Sister Mary Felicia into the golf cart.

Within a few minutes, they arrived at Leo's enclosure. Jaime parked in one of the designated spots and escorted them to another part of the enclosure where Charlie was signing to Leo. Leo was behind a glass window in a covered walkway, where people could walk and watch the animals. It was still early, so the usual crowds had not yet arrived. Charlie used a tissue to wipe at her eyes between signing to Leo.

Charlie turned around when she heard the trio make their way to the enclosure. She shook her head, her eyes reddened and swollen from crying. "I'm so glad you're here. We're so worried about Leo. He won't drink or eat anything."

"Has he communicated anything to you?" asked Jaime.

Leo stared at them as they gathered around. Sister Maggie noticed he held a rubber toy in the shape of a duck in his hand.

"Sam gave Leo that toy," Jaime said. "He won't put it down. He's also signing over and over again, 'Leo-sad, Leo-cry, call-Papa-Sam.'"

"Papa is Leo's name for Sam." Charlie heaved a deep, shuddering sigh. "Sam was like his father. He meant so much to him and—to all of us."

"Leo could be feeding off your grief right now," suggested Sister Maggie, reaching out to give the young woman's hand a gentle squeeze. "Perhaps we might try to stay calm when we're in his line of vision. Leo is very intuitive and will pick up on our facial expressions and tone of voice."

Charlie gaped for a moment and then a flicker of awareness lit her eyes. "Of course. You're very wise, Sister Maggie." She wiped her eyes, blew her nose, and took a deep breath." Of course, my obvious distress is visible to Leo and making him more anxious."

"I wonder if you'll permit me to try to communicate with Leo after Sister Mary Felicia sings to him?"

Sister Mary Felicia moved next to Charlie and touched her shoulder. "I'd like to sing Leo's favorite song."

Charlie nodded. "He'll like that."

"Go for it," Jaime said.

Charlie moved aside, and Sister Mary Felicia stood face to face with Leo. He immediately took notice of her and signed.

Charlie laughed. "He wants you to sing the monkey song."

Sister Mary Felicia removed the guitar strap from her shoulder and positioned the instrument in front of her to play. Leo moved up to the glass, staring at the guitar in fascination.

"You have his complete attention," remarked Sister Maggie.

Sister Mary Felicia began to strum the guitar. "I've changed the song a bit," said the young nun. "The nursery rhyme is now about ten orangutans jumping on the bed." Then she sang until the last of the orangutans fell off the bed.

Leo slapped his huge hand against the cement floor and fell to his side in what appeared to be a giggling fit. He clearly enjoyed Sister Mary Felicia's rendition of the nursery rhyme.

They all chuckled when he signed to Charlie, "more," and Charlie signed to Leo that Sister Mary would sing again but that Sister Maggie wanted to say hello too.

Leo regarded Sister Maggie and pointed to her neck again. Her silver crucifix picked up the natural sunlight and sparkled as she held it up for Leo to see.

"Hi, Leo. How are you today?" asked Sister Maggie as she approached the glass separating them. She held up her crucifix, and he stared at it. Charlie signed Sister Maggie's question when Leo looked up. He signed back, "Leo-sad, Leo-cry."

"Can you ask Leo why he's sad?"

Charlie signed the question to Leo. She then interpreted Leo's signs. "Leo-sad, Leo-cry, Papa-draped."

"Does Leo understand death?" Sister Maggie asked. "Is that what Papa-draped means? He knows Sam won't be coming back?"

"When Sam worked at the New York State Zoo, an older female orangutan named Doris took a maternal interest in Leo," Jaime said. "She even allowed Leo to sleep with her. She groomed him, gave him affection, and even disciplined him when he misbehaved." Jaime quirked a sad smile. "About a year after Doris began to mother Leo, she passed away from heart disease. When Doris's body was removed from the enclosure, the zookeepers covered her with a sheet. That's when Leo identified death as being draped. But he still didn't make the connection about the finality of it all."

"I understand," replied Sister Maggie. "Leo watched as Doris was taken away under a shroud. That's very concrete, but he may have expected her to return."

"Yes, he did," Jaime said. "Sam told me Leo signed several times a day for Sam to bring Doris home. He did this for a few weeks, even though Sam kept explaining to him what had happened. It was as though Leo couldn't accept the truth, much like humans who are in a state of denial after the death of a loved one. Although we understand our loved one is gone, our emotions have a hard time coping. But with Leo, Doris's draping and absence launched him into major denial. Then one morning, Sam asked Leo where Doris went after she was draped, and Leo signed 'gone.'"

"Did Leo keep asking for Doris even after that?" Sister Mary Felicia asked.

"He sometimes did, and then Sam would remind him," Charlie said.

"One day, Sam asked Leo if he missed Doris," Jaime added. "Leo signed something that left a permanent impression on Sam. Leo signed 'Leo-love, Leo-love Doris, Doris-draped, Doris-sleep.' Remember, he watched as her body was removed from the enclosure. He saw she had been limp and unresponsive. He connected being draped with being asleep and unresponsive. When Doris never returned, Leo would always respond to Sam that Doris was asleep," said Jaime.

"Leo might be in that denial stage once again," Sister Maggie said. "Charlie, can you ask Leo if he thinks Papa-Sam is asleep like Doris?"

"Leo, where is Doris?" signed Charlie.

Leo signed, "asleep."

Charlie continued. "Is Papa Sam asleep?"

Leo paused. He signed over and over that she had to get Papa-Sam.

"That's so sad," Sister Mary Felicia said, a catch in her voice. "Even though he understands about Doris, he's unwilling or unable to make that connection about Sam. He's not ready to let him go."

Sister Maggie nodded. When the young woman lost her little brother in the car accident, it took her a long time before she could emotionally accept the heart-breaking loss. Which was why the rituals surrounding a family member or friend's death were important, Sister Maggie thought. It helped the mind and heart to say good-bye and to begin to heal. Sister Maggie and her family never had that chance with Catie. She swallowed the sudden lump that formed in her throat. *Will we ever have that chance?* She hoped so. She shook off her sad thoughts and turned to Charlie once more. "Charlie, can you ask Leo who made Papa-Sam fall down?"

No sooner had Charlie asked the question than Leo became agitated. He signed the same thing over and over again. "Bad man, Papa fall."

"Can you ask Leo what he saw the bad man do?" asked Sister Maggie.

"Bad man, bad water stick," Charlie said, as Leo gestured.

"Water stick means gun," she explained. "About a month ago, Sam gave Leo a water gun to play with outside. Leo learned how to use it and got a kick out of spraying Sam. Unfortunately, Leo decided to aim it at Dr. Souter as he was passing by with several zoo donors. And that was the end of the water stick."

Leo kept signing to Charlie that she should call Papa-Sam.

When Charlie signed nothing back, Leo turned his back on the three women.

"Maybe it's time to offer up that little treat to Leo," Sister Mary Felicia suggested.

"I agree," Sister Maggie added. "Leo's been most helpful today, and despite what Dr. Souter says, a little comfort food in moderation never hurt anyone."

"Did you bring Leo a Stack-Five Burger?" Charlie asked Jaime.

Jaime nodded as his face flushed. "I thought it might help."

Charlie went to the other side of the glass enclosure so Leo could see her signing to him. "Leo, do you want a meat-cheese-bread?"

To everyone's amazement, Leo continued to ignore everyone.

"Wow. This is a first for Leo to reject his favorite treat," Charlie said.

"Let me try something." Sister Mary Felicia moved closer to the enclosure with her guitar. She began to strum and hum. Leo immediately turned around and listened intently.

Sister Maggie had never heard the tune before, but knowing how talented Sister Mary Felicia was, she was no doubt writing songs for the Christian music record she was working on. When Sister Mary Felicia performed at the singing competition last year in New York City, a record producer approached her backstage, knowing she was the former Casey Bauer, a budding pop star ten years before. He had read about the tragic circumstances of her leaving the industry. After Sister Mary Felicia's performance, the producer asked to meet with her and in the following weeks offered her a recording contract.

Sister Maggie asked Charlie to sign to Leo one more question about the identity of the man who made Sam fall down and get draped. "Can you ask Leo if the man with the water stick was a zookeeper or someone who worked here?" Sister Maggie directed.

"He may turn his back on us again," said Charlie as she signed the question. Charlie explained Leo understood that zookeepers were humans who worked at the Indiana State Zoo. He knew who they were partly because of what they did but also because of what they wore. They all dressed as Sam did. And besides, Leo knew all the zookeepers.

Leo signed back that the bad man was not a zookeeper.

"Well, I guess we know the killer was someone outside the zoo," concluded Sister Maggie. "Leo has certainly helped us figure that out."

"Amazing," Sister Mary Felicia said. "Leo was a witness to the murder."

"But it still leaves the field of suspects wide open," Jaime said. "It could have been anyone."

"No, not anyone," Sister Maggie stressed. "This was not a random act of violence. The man who killed Sam knew him. He definitely had a motive. Not to mention, Sam was shot execution-style. So, this was planned and executed down to the last detail."

"How do you know so much about all this crime stuff?" Jaime asked.

"I have assisted the police a few times," Sister Maggie replied.

"Sister Maggie's dad was a police captain, and three of her brothers work in law enforcement," Sister Mary Felicia said. "You might say, she's got a knack for sleuthing."

"Well, we certainly appreciate your coming here today," Charlie said. "I think the police need all the help they can get."

"Interesting the cops didn't think of interviewing Leo," Jaime mused as he walked around the glass enclosure. He delivered the delectable burger by a wooden door with an open slat to Leo, who didn't hesitate this time.

"Well, they likely didn't even consider it," Sister Maggie said. "In fact, they have no idea Leo might very well be their star witness."

Leo began to sign again, this time with ferocious intensity.

"What is he saying?" asked Sister Maggie, wondering if Leo had remembered something more from last night.

"Leo is signing that he wants another meat-cheese-bread now," Charlie replied. "He keeps emphasizing right now." Despite her grief, she began to laugh. "Not only that, but he wants me to get the keys so the song lady can join him in the enclosure."

CHAPTER NINE

April 20, 12:30 p.m.
Woodbury Animal Clinic
Indianapolis, Indiana

"WHAT AN ADORABLE KITTEN," Charlie remarked as she lifted Courtney out of the polka-dotted pink carrier onto the examining table. "Isn't she darling, Dale?" Charlie asked as her husband smiled and rubbed the sides of the black kitten's cheeks.

"My wife said Sister Mary Felicia found her hiding outside by the rectory garage," Dale Wells said as he began his formal examination of the kitten. "For a street cat, she seems very healthy, alert, and intelligent. By the way, where is Sister Mary Felicia?"

"We drove in from New Hope together. I dropped her off at her cousin Jaime's apartment so they could have a visit. Jaime's very upset about the death of his good friend, Sam."

In addition to blood work, Dale told Sister Maggie he would also vaccinate the kitten against the usual feline diseases. "She'll need to be spayed. You can bring her back once we have all her blood tests back. Charlie can schedule the spaying."

Charlie pulled out a cat toy to entertain Courtney as Dale gathered what he needed.

"Charlie mentioned you once worked at St. Malachy's parish in Brooklyn," Dale said.

"Are you familiar with the parish?" asked Sister Maggie, rubbing Courtney behind the ears to help keep her calm.

"I grew up in the neighborhood. My father, Dale Wells Senior, and my mother, Maria Rosales-Wells, owned a grocery store that specialized in Latino food products."

"Was it called *Comida Latina?* It was closed by the time I was sent to St. Malachy's," Sister Maggie said. "But I remember parishioners talking about it and how much they missed the products sold there."

Charlie held the cat on the lab table as Dale drew blood samples. "That would be the store," Dale replied, setting aside the small tubes. "My parents moved and sold the property. They ended up opening *Wells Sporting Goods* on Queens Boulevard. My father always boasted that his family came from the great state of Texas. Dad liked to characterize himself as the rugged, outdoors type. He loved hunting and camping, both of which my mother despises to this day."

Sister Maggie cocked her head. "You speak of your father in the past tense."

"My father died in a hunting accident about five years ago. He moved into the line of fire and was shot by another deer hunter."

"Dale's father passed away from surgical complications," added Charlie.

Sister Maggie could see Dale didn't want to elaborate on the accident as he focused his attention on giving Courtney her shots.

"By the way, I am familiar with your father's sporting goods store in Queens. My brothers and I went there a few years back to purchase camping gear for a family vacation. I recall my brother John also bought a Mossberg. It's a nice rifle for the price. One of Johnny's favorites for hunting."

Dale raised his eyebrows at Sister Maggie's easy reference to the rifle.

"My dad was a police captain, and my brothers work in law

enforcement, so I grew up around guns and rifles." Sister Maggie smiled. "My brothers are avid hunters, too. I can't say I enjoy the sport, but Johnny's venison stew certainly hits the spot on a cold, snowy day."

"You are full of surprises," Dale replied, petting a now-sleeping Courtney. "My dad was a gun aficionado as well."

"Dale inherited his father's collection of guns," Charlie said. "You had them appraised a few years back, didn't you, honey?"

"I sure did, and I've got the papers to prove it. They're worth a pretty penny, actually. I'm lucky to have the collection."

"While I'm happy the collection has sentimental and monetary value, I'm also glad those guns and rifles are all locked away," Charlie said. "I'd be afraid to have children in the same room even if the bullets are in the safe." She went on to tell Sister Maggie that she and Dale were expecting a baby around Thanksgiving.

"Congratulations."

"Thank you," Charlie and Dale both said in unison. Dale grinned from ear to ear as he wrapped his arm around Charlie and hugged her close.

"I can understand your concern about keeping the collection stored away," Sister Maggie added. "My father kept all his firearms securely locked up."

"We couldn't agree more," Dale said. "Little Miss Courtney will be very sleepy for the rest of the day. Keep an eye on her in case she reacts to the shots. But she should be fine. If you have any issues, give us a call."

"I definitely will," Sister Maggie said.

"It was lovely meeting you, Sister Maggie. I wish we could chat longer, but duty calls. I have a Pekinese named Bugsy waiting for me next door." Dale shook hands with Sister Maggie. "I'll see you again in a week or so." He turned to Charlie. "No charge for the Adorers of Divine Love."

"Thank you so much, Dale."

"Not a problem. You're doing God's work and taking care of God's creatures." He gave them a wink as he left the examination room.

Charlie helped Sister Maggie put Courtney back in the carrier and escorted her out to her car. "That was most kind of your husband. Please thank him again."

"Dale has a heart of gold. Especially when it comes to animals," Charlie said as she held the cat carrier while Sister Maggie opened the back door.

"Does Dale speak Spanish as well?" Sister Maggie asked as Charlie handed her the carrier.

"He's bilingual. His Colombian mother is a first-generation American." She laughed. "Most people have no idea Dale has a Latino heritage. He looks very Anglo since he's the spitting image of his late father." Charlie gave Sister Maggie a business card. "Just call when you want to schedule Courtney's spaying. I'm here every Saturday."

Sister Maggie thanked her again. Charlie waved, then jogged back into the clinic.

As Sister Maggie drove off, she wondered if Dale knew Father O'Connor, the pastor at St. Malachy's parish in Brooklyn. She'd have to remember to ask Dale next time. Father O'Connor had been there for years before Sister Maggie arrived. He must have known him.

"It's a small world, isn't it, Courtney?" Sister Maggie smiled as she heard the soft meowing coming from the carrier.

She'd ask Father O'Connor tomorrow. He was turning 83, and she wanted to call him to wish him a happy birthday in any case.

"I'll kill two birds with one stone, as they say."

CHAPTER TEN

April 20, 12:45 p.m.
Condo of Jaime Bauer
Indianapolis, Indiana

"DID you tell the police that two truckers from King Cleaning Supplies attacked Sam a few days before his murder?" asked Sister Mary Felicia as she took a last sip of coffee, then set the cup in the sink in Jaime's small but sleek kitchen. Jaime lived in a new condo complex near the White River State Park. He was Mr. Modern when it came to his home and his décor. Definitely not the cozy, shabby chic look Sister Mary Felicia liked but then again, Jaime always liked modern everything.

"I sure did. I also told them that Sam identified them as Mitchel Fowler and Dylan King, the white supremacists he knew in college from the Alliance of Heritage Nationalists," Jaime said. He tucked his blue, no-button polo shirt into beige pants. "Are you sure you want to do this? You told Sister Maggie you were coming over here to hang out with me today."

Sister Mary Felicia blushed as she picked up her purse. "I'm sure Sister Maggie won't mind we're doing a bit of sleuthing for her.

Besides, I can't wait to see her face when you drive me back to the convent, and we tell her later."

"She'll probably hassle you for going."

"Yes, and then she'll grill me on everything we find out," Sister Mary Felicia said.

"Okay, where is this warehouse anyway?" Jaime asked as he led the way to the underground parking garage where he parked his silver Prius.

Sister Mary Felicia scrolled down on her cell phone. "The warehouse for King Cleaning Supplies is on North Bedford, about a fifteen-minute drive from here."

"All righty then, Sister Columbo. Let's go."

As they drove to the warehouse, Sister Mary Felicia turned to her cousin. "Sister Maggie mentioned the manager should have work logs. Those logs should reveal the whereabouts of Fowler and King around the time Sam was murdered."

"Did Sister Maggie intend to sneak into the warehouse after hours to snoop around or something?" Jaime asked with a grin.

"Knowing Sister Maggie, probably yes."

"So we're doing the sneaking around for her, instead."

"I just want to help," Sister Mary Felicia said. "Besides, it's Saturday, so I doubt the place will be closed. It's a cleaning supply building, so they must be open six days a week."

"Well, maybe we can find something out, in any case."

"Tell me again about that day when Sam was assaulted. You mentioned King Cleaning wasn't the usual supplier? But the zoo was trying them out?"

"Yes, the zoo had had a few issues with the previous company so the operations manager had been in touch with King Cleaning."

"And they were there that day delivering supplies?" Sister Mary Felicia asked.

"Yeah, it was a routine thing. But it all went off the rails," Jaime replied. "Juan Espinoza, the zookeeper you met at the fundraiser, was rounding the corner when he saw Mitch Fowler pin Sam's arms behind his back. Juan started running toward them as Dylan King punched Sam in the gut. Juan pepper-sprayed Fowler, who fell to the ground. That's when I arrived on the scene and jumped in to help. King tried to make a run for the truck, but Juan and I managed to drag him down to the ground. Sam got back up, and he helped Juan hold down King while I called security. Fowler was out of commission from the pepper spray."

"Were they arrested?" Sister Mary Felicia asked.

"No. Which we found odd. Security was going to call in the police and Sam said he didn't want to press charges. That it was all a misunderstanding. The security guards were as surprised as Juan and I were. But Sam insisted. So the guards told King and Fowler to leave and never come back or they would definitely call the cops next time. As King took the wheel of the truck, he called out to Sam and held up his right hand like a gun and pointed it at Sam. They tore out of there after that," said Jaime. "The security guards just shook their heads and said they would note what happened in their report to the head of security. The head would then decide if there would be any follow-up."

"But why did Sam refuse to press charges?" Sister Mary Felicia asked.

"After the incident, Sam told me the two men were nothing but thugs. He said he knew them from years back when he'd joined the AHN as a freshman at Danfield College. Sam eventually smartened up and left the AHN and its cause. He didn't want to press charges because he wanted no future contact with them and simply wanted Fowler and King out of his life."

"Sam was a white supremacist? I would never have suspected," said Sister Mary Felicia with a frown. She'd make sure to tell Sister Maggie everything when Jaime drove her back to the convent.

"He was a complicated man. He may have been a lot of things, but I can assure you Sam wasn't a racist. He loved animals and was a dedicated conservationist. In his relationships with people, however, he made some pretty bad choices over the years. I'll spare you the details," stressed Jaime.

"Do you think the two men who attacked Sam carried a grudge

against him after all these years because he quit their lousy organization?" Sister Mary Felicia asked.

"The grudge goes much deeper," Jaime said. "Before Sam went to Borneo, he was a prosecuting attorney. His last case involved a murder trial that was racially motivated. Mitch Fowler and Dylan King were accused of killing a civil rights protestor. Sam had to recuse himself because of his past connection with the men."

"Sister Maggie mentioned that to me after Sam's murder. Juan told her about it during the fundraising dinner."

"It was a big mess," Jaime said. "Even though he'd come clean and recused himself, it was too late, Sam had been the original prosecutor on the case, and the defense used it to their advantage. Sam's desire to make up for his past went down the tubes. He wanted to get as far away from his past as he could, so he sold everything, packed up, and went to Borneo, where he got a job working in animal conservation. The rest is history," Jaime said.

"That's a complicated life for sure," Sister Mary Felicia said. She glanced at her GPS app. "The King Warehouse should be after the next right."

A minute later, Jaime pulled into the parking lot. They got out of the car and went inside. The manager's office was at the end of the hall. A sign on the door read: "Go Away! No One Cares!"

"Sounds like a gem of a boss." Sister Mary Felicia arched her brows as she knocked on the door.

"Come in," growled a deep voice from inside.

An older balding man in dungarees and sweatshirt stood up. "What can I do for you?"

Jaime stepped forward and introduced himself and Sister Mary Felicia. "I work for the Indiana State Zoo. Two of your drivers delivered cleaning supplies the other day. One of our zookeepers was attacked by them. The gentleman who was attacked asked our security team not to contact the authorities. But they have reported the incident to the management and will most likely be getting in touch with you soon, if they haven't already. I can report back to them and inform them what disciplinary actions you've taken against Mitchel Fowler and Dylan King.

"Disciplinary actions? This ain't no middle school, boy. It's likely your zookeeper friend provoked the fight."

Sister Mary Felicia looked at the name on the metal desk plate: Frank King. She cleared her throat. "Mr. King, might you be the father of Dylan King, the driver?"

"Best son in the world," King replied. "Does the zoo plan to press charges against my son and Mitch Fowler, or against King Cleaning Supplies? I'd like to know in case I need to contact our lawyers. Otherwise, you and the cute little nun should leave my warehouse, or I'll call the cops and have you charged with trespassing."

Jaime and Sister Mary Felicia exchanged a glance. Jaime turned back to King. "It was a nice meeting you," he said sarcastically. Jaime took Sister Mary Felicia's arm as they left the office.

When they got back to their car, Jaime chuckled.

"Is there something amusing about our exchange with Mr. King?" asked Sister Mary Felicia.

"I can't wait for you to tell Sister Maggie about our encounter with Frank King," replied Jaime. "I can only imagine what Sister Maggie would have said to him had she been here."

Sister Mary Felicia cocked her head as she glanced at her cousin. "Oh, she would have let him have it with both barrels. Sister Maggie never minces words, especially around ignorant people. She'd have had him shaking in his boots."

"Did you notice his name plate?" Jaime asked. "Frank King. He owns the company."

"Owner or not, Sister Maggie would have blasted him with a lecture about equal rights and racial equality," Sister Mary Felicia added.

"Did you see that X-rated calendar hanging on the wall behind his desk?"

"What am I, blind?" Sister Mary Felicia huffed out. "Of course, I saw it. A nude woman posing in front of a red pickup truck," Sister Mary Felicia rolled her eyes.

"Sister Maggie would have lectured him about that too," Jaime said.

"She would have asked him if that was his daughter posing in her birthday suit," added Sister Mary Felicia. "That would have started an interesting exchange." She snapped her seat belt. She couldn't wait to get back to the convent to let Sister Maggie know how their little visit with Frank King had gone.

"We still have a lot of learning to do before we get as good as Sister Maggie, P.I." Jaime's eyes narrowed and he sat forward. "Look. The prodigal son and his bestie are back." He pointed to Dylan King and Mitch Fowler, who were crossing the parking lot. "That's King's son on the phone," Jaime said. "I bet he's chatting with Frank."

Sister Mary Felicia saw Dylan King bobbing his head like a buoy bouncing in choppy waters as he spoke. A loud peal of thunder sounded, followed by a flash of lightning. "Let's get out of here before the downpour starts," she said.

Jaime put the car in reverse and pulled out of the parking lot.

Sister Mary Felicia glanced over her shoulder—and saw both Dylan and Mitch getting into a glossy red pickup truck. She wondered if it was the same truck on the calendar and if that was why he'd bought it. Guys like that were always looking for a status symbol or the flashiest car to impress women. Despite her youth and naïveté when she had her first hit single at 16 after winning the American Star competition, Sister Mary Felicia, or Casey as she'd been known back then, had had her parents to guide her. Sadly, she'd witnessed many an aspiring female singer fall for sleazy men who promised them the moon.

By the time Jaime turned onto the highway on-ramp, it was pouring rain, and he flicked on the windshield wipers and slowed his speed accordingly.

Sister Mary Felicia's instinct made her glance back over her shoulder. She spotted the red pickup truck behind them, too close for comfort. "Be careful, Jaime. I think King and Fowler are following us."

"What?" Jaime glanced into the rear-view mirror.

"Keep your eyes peeled ahead, Jaime," Sister Mary Felicia warned. "The roads will be getting slick pretty fast because of the rain."

"How do you know they're behind us?"

"I saw them get into that red pickup truck parked outside the building as we were heading out."

"Why didn't you tell me?"

"Because you were fighting the road in bad weather. Besides, I didn't think they would tail us. I thought they were going their own way."

"Maybe they just happen to be driving in the same direction we are," Jaime countered, flicking the wipers on high. The rain came down in sheets, and Sister Mary Felicia was getting a crick in her neck as she strained to look behind her.

"I doubt that. Just please be careful and keep your eyes on the road. I'll keep my eye on them."

A few minutes later, the huge pickup truck pulled up alongside Jaime's silver Prius and then suddenly slammed into the driver's side.

Sister Mary Felicia screamed. "Why are they doing this?"

"Hang on," Jaime said.

Sister Mary Felicia prayed the brutes were only trying to scare them and would drive off. But when they rammed into them again, she pulled out her phone and called 911. As she told the operator what was going on, the pickup truck side-swiped them a third time. Sister Mary Felicia dropped the phone as the car went into a tailspin and skidded onto a grassy area with trees and bushes. She screamed as the car barreled toward a tall pole, her last conscious thought was a prayer to God to help them.

CHAPTER ELEVEN

April 20, 2:30 p.m.
St. Barnabas Hospital
Indianapolis, Indiana

If there was one phone call Sister Maggie dreaded getting, it was a call from the hospital. "How are they?" she asked the ER nurse.

"Sister Mary Felicia is in an exam room being attended to. Her cousin, Jaime Bauer, gave us your number to contact you."

Sister Maggie had received the urgent call just as she was unloading the cat carrier from the car. She'd rushed into the house and left Courtney with Sister Ruthie while Sister Rose Marie, a nurse practitioner, offered to accompany her to St. Barnabas Hospital in Indianapolis.

Sister Maggie punched the cell phone's speaker on and handed it to Sister Rose Marie as the two women rushed to the car.

"Can you give us any details about their condition, Elvira?" Sister Rose Marie knew the ER nurse well since they'd worked at the same hospital before Elvira moved to Indianapolis.

"Sister Mary Felicia suffered a concussion and is unconscious," Elvira replied. They're examining her now, but I promise to let you know as soon as I can. I'll pop back there in a bit when I get a chance and check with Samantha. She's the nurse attending Sister Mary Felicia."

"Thank you so much," Sister Rose Marie said.

Sister Maggie's hand immediately went to the cross hanging around her neck. "Is Jaime okay?"

"Jaime wanted me to reassure you he's doing fine," Elvira said. "He broke his arm in three places from the impact of the crash. A cast is being applied to his arm as we speak. I'll make sure to have them bring him here when they're done."

"Did either of them say anything about the crash?" asked Sister Maggie.

"They were pretty woozy when the paramedics wheeled them in," Elvira said. "Officer Mills was on the scene and followed the ambulance here. I believe he's still here waiting to speak with Jaime about the accident."

"Officer Mills—do you mean Stewart Mills?" Sister Maggie asked. "Officer Mills' parents are members of our parish in New Hope. We know their son quite well." Sister Maggie thought highly of the young officer. He'd only been on the Indianapolis Metropolitan Police Department for about five years, but he'd proven himself a level-headed officer with the intuition and insight of a seasoned detective.

"Yes, that's him. He's a friend—I mean to say—he's here quite a bit because he covers the highway as part of his route. Jaime told him they were forced off the road by another vehicle and crashed into an electrical pole."

"Oh, my goodness," Sister Rose Marie said, and her lips moved in a silent prayer.

Sister Maggie blinked back tears, trying not to let the shock of it all overwhelm her. She needed answers.

"I doubt we'll get a chance to speak with him," Sister Maggie added. "We are heading out from New Hope and should be there within the hour."

"When you arrive at St. Barnabas, you can sit in the waiting area. I suspect it's likely going to be a few hours before we hear anything, given how busy we are."

Sister Maggie and Sister Rose Marie thanked Elvira and began their drive to Indianapolis.

****

WHEN SISTERS MAGGIE and Rose Marie finally arrived at St. Barnabas Hospital, they entered the waiting room and spotted two empty seats in the corner. They sat down, and both sighed.

"I wonder if the other vehicle drove them off the road by accident because of the weather," Sister Rose Marie said. "It seems odd, though, that they were driving on the highway. Didn't Sister Mary Felicia say she was going to spend some time at Jaime's place because he was so distraught about Sam's death?"

"Yes, but I have a feeling they were up to something," Sister Maggie added.

"Do you think they were sleuthing?"

"I'm afraid so."

"Well, all we can do for now is to pray and wait. We'll get answers soon enough."

Sister Maggie nodded, but inside she was worried the pair's activities may have been connected to the crash. She prayed that Sister Mary Felicia and Jaime were going to be all right. She also couldn't help the wave of guilt gripping her insides like a claw. If it weren't for her own amateur detective work, Sister Mary Felicia might not have been inspired to try her hand at sleuthing. There were times when Sister Maggie questioned her need to uncover the truth when it came to crimes, especially murder. Yes, she grew up in a law enforcement family and, at one point, had considered becoming a police officer, but then she took on her calling of becoming a religious sister, and she loved it. So why all the sleuthing?

Catie. Yes, it had to be her sister. When Catie had gone missing all those years ago, thirteen-year-old Maureen was beyond devastated. But beyond that, she became obsessed with finding out what had happened. She collected newspaper clippings, did research on the area, and as she got older, she'd pick her dad's brain about investigative techniques. She even got a summer job working at the local library so she could learn more about research methods. Every lunch break she'd pore over volumes of textbooks about missing person investigations to see if she could find an approach or possible lead the police had missed. As a teenager, she'd wondered if her dad had given up much too soon. She didn't tell her parents that, of course, because she knew how devasted they were over Catie's abduction. Eventually, with the help of Sister Mary Christine at their church, she let go of her own obsession. Still, she couldn't bear to destroy all the information she'd accumulated, so she'd boxed it all up and stored it in her parents' attic.

After her mother sold the house to move into her assisted living apartment, Sister Maggie stored her research at the motherhouse where she stored some things from her childhood, things she couldn't take with her on her missions because she moved every five years or so. But one day, she promised herself, she would go through everything and put the past to rest.

"Sister Maggie!"

She looked up and saw Jaime in a wheelchair waving at her and Sister Rose Marie. They stood up as the orderly wheeled Jaime over.

"Thanks, Clyde." Jaime, being the PR fellow that he was, introduced Clyde the orderly to them. "I'm going to wait here with my friends while Sister Mary Felicia is being looked after."

"No problem, Jaime," Clyde said. "Holler if you need me."

"Will do. Thanks, man," Jaime shook hands with Clyde, who smiled at Sister Maggie and Sister Rose Marie, then walked back through the sliding glass doors to where patients were either waiting to see doctors or having tests.

"How are you feeling, Jaime?" Sister Rose Marie asked as she examined Jaime's cast, hand, and fingers.

"You must be the nurse practitioner my cousin told me about," Jaime said. "I'm okay. It's Casey I'm worried about."

"Do you know anything about her condition?" asked Sister Maggie.

"I asked Clyde to wheel me past her on our way out. She was in one of the rooms waiting for her imaging results. They're concerned about her concussion. The nurse had given Casey something for the pain. She was pretty groggy. She's waiting to see the doctor again after they get the scans back to see if she can go home or if they need to admit her."

"Thank God, you're both alive. Tell us what happened," Sister Maggie said.

"We were run off the road," Jaime said in a low voice. He glanced around as though to make sure no one was within earshot. "Mitch Fowler and Dylan King deliberately tried to kill us."

"Wait a minute. Back it up. Who are these guys, and why did they go after the two of you?" Sister Maggie asked.

"They went to the same college as Sam in freshman year," Jaime replied. "They talked Sam into joining a group called the AHN, the Alliance of Heritage Nationalists, and when Sam finally came to his senses and rejected their white supremacy ideology, he tried to leave. They beat him up for daring to get away, and he had to transfer to another college for his own safety. The day before your zoo tour, King Cleaning delivered supplies, and Fowler and King were the drivers. They spotted Sam and started punching him before, one of the zookeepers, Juan Espinoza, and I came along and stopped them."

Sister Maggie was shocked by the information. Yet, part of her wasn't really surprised. Sam appeared to be a complicated man and a magnet for trouble. "Rather than telling the police, you and Sister Felicia decided to take matters into your own hands?"

"We called security at the time, but Sam refused to press charges." Jaime paused, rubbing his good hand across his face. "To be honest, Casey and I did something stupid, and I blame myself. We went to King Cleaning Supplies to find out if the warehouse manager had a work log for Fowler and King on the day Sam was killed. It would prove they'd made a run to the zoo that day and might have been enough for the police to question the two men. Unfortunately, we discovered too late that King Cleaning Supplies is owned by Frank King, Dylan's father."

"I imagine any questions about his son were not well-received," said Sister Rose Marie.

"Charm ranks low on his list of personality traits. When he realized we were digging for facts about his son and Fowler, he ordered us out and threatened to call the police to report us as trespassers. As we left, we saw him take out his phone and make a call. He must have called his son because I saw Junior on his phone in the parking lot. Fowler was right beside him. Then Casey saw Junior and Fowler get into a red pickup truck as we were leaving."

"Did they hit you from behind or cut you off?" Sister Rose Marie asked. "It was pouring rain. You both must have been terrified."

"Oh, we were scared, all right. They actually sideswiped us several times. I tried to outrun them, but my Prius was no match for that monster truck."

Sister Maggie imagined Sister Mary Felicia and Jaime confronting Frank King. She shook her head. *I wish I'd been there. We could have handled things without ruffling feathers. Then again, knowing the group those thugs belong to and their history with Sam, it could have very well turned out the same.*

"Jaime, Sister Rose Marie, will you excuse me? I have to make a phone call. Will you both be sitting here for a while?"

"Yes, of course," Sister Rose Marie replied. "We'll text you if we hear anything about Sister Mary Felicia."

Sister Maggie walked to a quiet spot just outside the entrance to the emergency room. She scrolled through her contacts until she found the name she was looking for and pressed dial.

"Jose Torres, speaking. How may I help you?"

"Jose, it's Sister Maggie Donovan. I need a huge favor from you."

"Sister Maggie, of course, what can I do for you?"

Sister Maggie almost sighed with relief. Jose Torres was her old friend from East New York, Brooklyn, from her days when she served at St. Malachy Parish. Back then, he was a detective as well as a parishioner at St. Malachy, he also covered the area in his job. Jose and his wife Marisol Cisneros met when they were just kids in the Sunday school class Sister Maggie taught for many years. They married right after college and had one son, named Angel. Marisol was still involved in the church and various charitable organizations while Jose was now Deputy Commissioner of Strategic Initiatives for the NYPD. Just the man for the job.

"I'm looking for a local contact regarding an attempted murder. Two men deliberately ran Sister Mary Felicia and her cousin, Jaime, off the highway."

"I'm so sorry," Jose replied. "As far as a local contact, let me handle that. My organization has been keeping our eye on the uptick of firearms and explosives being circulated through Indianapolis in the past few months. We're working with IMPD already."

The Lord works in mysterious ways, she thought. "They were sideswiped multiple times by a red pickup truck probably owned by a man named Mitch Fowler or Dylan King. Or perhaps Frank King, the father of Dylan King. They're employed by King Cleaning Supplies, owned by Frank King."

"Got it," Jose said. "Can you give me any other details?"

Sister Maggie gave him a run-down of everything that had happened from Sam's murder, including his history with Fowler and King and their connection to the AHN, to the car crash.

"I wouldn't be surprised if King Cleaning Supplies is a conduit for other criminal activities in Indianapolis," said Sister Maggie. "Sister Mary Felicia and her cousin had no idea what nasty people they were dealing with when they went fishing for information. King Senior is no fish. He's a barracuda."

"I'll get on this ASAP. And thanks for the tip," Jose said. "We've seen a crossover between these groups and incidents of domestic terrorism."

"Can you also make contact with Officer Stewart Mills? He was the officer on duty who showed up on the scene. I know him personally, and he's a good man. We missed him by ten minutes here at the hospital."

"Will do, Sister Maggie."

"Thanks, Jose, I owe you one."

"By the way, Sister Maggie, when are you coming home for a visit? We missed you last time you were here, but I heard about what happened with your goddaughter from Jimmy Rizzo."

"That was a doozy of a time, let me tell you." Sister Maggie heard the deep rumble of laughter coming through the phone.

"Whenever there's trouble, you're usually in there taking care of business, aren't you, Sister Maggie?"

"Next time I get back to Brooklyn, I'll stop by for a good catch-up."

"Maria would love to make you her famous *asopao de pollo*."

"I can't turn that down, can I?"

"Don't even try."

CHAPTER TWELVE

April 20, 4:40 p.m.
St. Barnabas Hospital
Indianapolis

SISTER MAGGIE SAT beside the hospital bed and prayed her rosary. Sister Rose Marie had driven Jaime home, despite his protests at wanting to stay at the hospital and wait for Sister Mary Felicia to wake up. Jaime could barely keep his eyes open after having been given painkillers, so Sister Rose Marie won that tug-of-war.

Sister Maggie smiled to herself. Poor Jaime didn't stand a chance with Sister Rose Marie. Both nuns had discussed bringing Jaime back to New Hope and putting him up in the convent's guestroom for a few days. Being in an empty apartment in his condition was unwise, and they also worried the hoodlums who ran him off the road might track him down. Plus, their plan got him back to his apartment to pack a few necessities.

Sister Maggie did get a chance to speak to Officer Mills. At Elvira's request, he returned to the hospital when he went off duty to meet with Sister Maggie. He gave her more details, including the condition of Jaime's car, which was now a heap of scrap. The young officer said they were lucky to be alive. *Amen to that.*

Sister Maggie briefed Stewart about her phone call to Jose. Stewart nodded and said he would also contact Jose about the accident and some observations of his own regarding the cleaning company. Stewart told her the police had begun watching the warehouse last week after getting an anonymous tip about possible suspicious activity in the middle of the night. Sister Maggie wondered if Sam had tipped them off. And if the Kings had located Sam deliberately. There were so many connections at play that Sister Maggie knew she'd need a good night's sleep to figure it all out.

A soft groan came from Sister Mary Felicia, drawing Sister Maggie's attention. She reached for the young woman's hand and held it between her own. The white bandage wrapped around the young sister's head and the IV bag above the bed reminded her of her own head injury after being attacked and trapped in a burning brownstone by the same men who'd terrorized her goddaughter and had been responsible for several murders.

Now that Sister Mary Felicia was resting comfortably, Sister Maggie decided to wait to update her parents until the morning. That would be soon enough, and Sister Mary Felicia could talk to them when she felt more herself.

A quote from Albert Einstein came to mind. "The world is a dangerous place to live, not because of the people who are evil, but because of the people who don't do anything about it."

Sister Maggie felt her cell phone vibrate as the nurse came in to check Sister Mary Felicia's vitals. She excused herself and quietly exited the hospital room to respond to Jose Torres.

"Two officers, Joe De Marco, and his partner, Tracy Loughlin, located the red pickup truck of Dylan King as it drove into the King warehouse parking lot. They asked the duo to explain the dents and silver paint streaks on the passenger side of the truck. The two fools were higher than kites and said they had no idea how the silver paint got on the vehicle. Paint samples are being analyzed right now. The police are doing everything by the book," reported Jose.

"Were they arrested?" asked Sister Maggie.

"Wait, it gets better. When the two jerks got out of the truck, our officers saw drug paraphernalia and evidence of cocaine powder on the black vinyl seats. They found 5,000 grams of coke in a large open toolbox and arrested them for trafficking and distributing drugs. You know, there's a ten-year mandatory minimum penalty on the federal charge," Jose added.

"Great work to you and those officers." Sister Maggie would have whooped for joy, but she reminded herself she was in the hallway of a hospital. "What about Frank King? That warehouse probably contains contraband goods."

"Here's the beautiful part, Sister Maggie. As De Marco and Loughlin were arresting Fowler and King, the father came out waving a loaded gun. Apparently, he'd been watching everything in his office from the security camera that faced the parking lot. And the gun wasn't a typical gun, but one of those antique guns they sell at shows. The officers deescalated the situation, seized the gun, and learned later that he had an expired license to carry a firearm. Given the arrests associated with the drugs and firearms, the police should be granted a warrant from a judge to search the warehouse," said Jose.

"Great police work. Thank you for moving so swiftly on all of this," replied Sister Maggie.

"How's Sister Mary Felicia doing?" asked Jose.

"She's resting. Given the silver paint on the side of the truck proving they drove Jaime's car off the road, I'm sure you'll be able to add attempted homicide to their list of crimes. I wouldn't be surprised if they murdered Sam as well, on the orders of Frank King," Sister Maggie added.

"I'll keep you posted on that," Jose said. "Once those dim bulbs realize they have significant prison time to face, they may seek out plea deals or turn on each other. We might get full confessions out of them on all of it."

After a short pause, Jose added, "It looks like I'll need to come to Indy for a few days pretty soon. Maybe we could have lunch."

"I'll look forward to it."

Sister Maggie thanked Jose again and then remembered she needed to call Father O'Connor and ask him about Dale. So many St. Malachy connections.

"Hola, Sor Elena," Sister Maggie greeted Sister Elena, the pastoral associate at St. Malachy.

"Que Dios le bendiga," Sor Elena replied.

She returned the words of blessing and exchanged a few pleasantries with her.

Sor Elena mentioned Luis Garcia, the former owner of the neighborhood junkyard called El Perro, and the official fence in the area for stolen appliances and goods, had been going to Mass at St. Malachy on a regular basis.

"Luis is working hard at turning his life around," Sor Elena said. "You remember Luis's eldest nephew, Javier, yes?"

"Yes, of course, I do. Is everything all right with the boy?" Sister Maggie recalled the well-mannered youth who'd come to visit her with his uncle Luis, bringing her a dish of homemade pernil his mother had made. He was definitely a sweet boy with a promising future.

"He is all right, but he was shot by a gang member a few weeks ago. Luckily it went clear through his shoulder and missed his heart."

"Oh, my goodness," Sister Maggie said. "How is the family doing?"

"Everyone was shaken up, especially Luis. You recall Luis had vowed to turn a corner and leave his life of crime behind. Well, he was slipping back into his old ways. But when Javier got shot, it reaffirmed his faith to change."

"I am heartened to hear it," Sister Maggie said. "So, no more junkyard and dealing in stolen goods?"

"Definitely not," Sor Elena replied. "Luis and his brother opened a Mexican restaurant downtown. Luis even feeds the homeless on a weekly basis with the meals from his restaurant. And they will be sending Javier to a private school so he will be away from the gangs."

Sister Maggie said a prayer of thanksgiving that they were all on the right path and thanked Sor Elena for updating her. *"Quiero hablar con el Padre O'Connor."*

Sor Elena promised she'd call with an update about Luis and Javier in a few weeks and then transferred her to Father O'Connor's line.

"Happy birthday, Father O'Connor. How does it feel to be 83?" asked Sister Maggie.

"About the same it felt to be 82," he said with a chuckle. "Truthfully, it seems like only yesterday I arrived at St. Malachy."

"Indeed, and praise God you're still there to continue your good works."

"Well, I can say it's never a dull moment. Are you in town?" asked the former exorcist of the Diocese of Brooklyn.

"No. I'm sending you my greetings from Indianapolis," Sister Maggie replied. "I just met a former parishioner of yours from St. Malachy. Do you remember Dale Wells Junior?"

"I certainly do. His mother, Maria Rosales-Wells, is still here in the parish. She volunteers at the rectory to prepare delicious Colombian meals a few times a month. Her husband is deceased."

"I was told he died in a hunting accident," Sister Maggie said.

"That's the official story," Father O'Connor replied.

"What do you mean?" Sister Maggie probed.

"Dale Senior was unfaithful to Maria. This is public knowledge, Clancy. Rumor has it he was shot by a jealous husband. He died in the hospital from sepsis and not the actual gunshot wound."

"How sad to grow up in a household where the father so disrespected his wife," said Sister Maggie. "If my father had been unfaithful, Mama Lulu would have made sure he suffered sufficiently for his crime."

Father O'Connor stifled a laugh. "I have no doubt Mama Lulu would have meted out justice. Maria, on the other hand, has always been about mercy and forgiveness. Dale Junior had a tumultuous relationship with his father growing up, and Maria often reminded her son that Jesus died on the cross for all sinners. She urged him to forgive his father and pray for his conversion."

"Extraordinary," Sister Maggie said.

"Indeed. The significant thing is that Dale Senior, on his deathbed, begged Maria's forgiveness for his infidelities. He did this in the presence of Dale Junior and medical personnel. Unfortunately, Dale Junior walked out of the room. I heard Dale Senior's last confession and gave him viaticum," said Father O'Connor.

Sister Maggie said her good-byes to Father O'Connor and promised to check in again with him soon. She then reflected on how children react to trauma in so many ways. She understood how sometimes forgiving and letting go were a challenge. Her thoughts returned to Dale, a talented veterinarian who clearly had a big heart when it came to animals. Sister Maggie hoped he could also find it in his heart to forgive his father and reconnect with this mother.

She heard a groan coming from Sister Mary Felicia's hospital room and hurried back in.

CHAPTER THIRTEEN

April 20, 5:00 p.m.
St. Barnabas Hospital,
Indianapolis, Indiana

"We were run off the road," Sister Mary Felicia whispered. "Did I get Jaime killed?" A tear ran down her cheek.

"He's all right." Sister Maggie sat in the chair by the bed. "Jaime broke his arm in the crash, but he's doing fine."

"Thank goodness," Sister Mary Felicia whispered. "I was so afraid."

"All is well with your cousin, dear. In fact, Sister Rose Marie drove him back to his apartment. We're determined to kidnap him for a few days with us in New Hope under the watchful eye of four very determined sisters."

Sister Mary Felicia smiled. "I'm glad he won't be alone tonight. Not with what he went through." They heard a quick knock, and the doctor stepped in.

"How are you, Sister Mary Felicia?"

"Feeling better," she replied with a wan smile.

"Do you remember me?" he asked.

"Yes, you're the doctor who examined me in the ER after my test results came back."

He covered his name tag.

"Do you remember my name?"

"Dr. Miguel Reyes."

"Excellent." Dr. Reyes introduced himself to Sister Maggie and told her she was welcome to stay as he examined Sister Mary Felicia. He checked her eyes and asked her to watch the beam from his penlight. Then he asked her more questions.

Sister Maggie was relieved that Sister Mary Felicia answered every question lucidly and with a clear memory. The poor girl was exhausted and banged up, but she was fully aware of everything and her memory was intact.

Dr. Reyes told them they admitted Sister Mary Felicia because she became unconscious at the scene of the accident. Then in the ER, she'd experienced some confusion when asked basic questions. "We found out this wasn't your first concussion," Dr. Reyes said. "Because of your earlier severe concussion, we wanted to take a few extra precautions, run a few more tests, and keep you in for the night. We'll be monitoring you carefully tonight, and if all seems well, you might be back home tomorrow."

"Has she had any seizures?" asked Sister Maggie.

"No. That doesn't mean it can't happen down the road. If that occurs, we can prescribe an anti-seizure medication—" The doctor's pager beeped. "I need to move on for now, but I'll check on you again tomorrow morning. The nurses will come in to see you every fifteen minutes throughout the night."

After Dr. Reyes had left, Sister Mary Felicia pressed the remote and lifted the head rest of her bed.

"I'm hungry."

"I think we missed the dinner service," Sister Maggie said. "Dina, your nurse, offered to bring us a couple of sandwiches earlier, but you were sound asleep, and I wanted to wait until you woke up. How about I grab something from the cafeteria? What would you like to eat?"

"I have a craving for a thick bacon burger with fries," Sister Mary Felicia said.

"It sounds like you're on the mend. If you'd asked for a tossed salad, I'd be suspicious," Sister Maggie said.

"That's for rabbits." She pulled a face.

Sister Maggie's cell phone rang, and she answered it.

"Hi Sister Maggie, it's Jaime."

"How are you doing?"

"Much better thanks to Sisters Rose Marie, Mary Frances, and Ruthie." He laughed. "I'm being well looked after..."

"What is he saying?" Sister Mary Felicia whispered anxiously.

"...Yes, she's right here," Sister Maggie said a few moments later. She handed Sister Mary Felicia the phone. "It's Jaime. He's feeling better and just told me he inhaled two huge bowls of homemade chicken noodle soup and two servings of vanilla and banana pudding. He wants to talk to you before heading to bed."

"Hi Jaime," the young woman said in a tearful voice. "I'm so sorry for almost getting you killed. It was all my fault. If I hadn't insisted on doing our sleuthing, you wouldn't be hurt."

Sister Maggie clucked her tongue like a mother hen and patted Sister Mary Felicia's knee as she continued to speak to Jaime. "Put him on speaker," Sister Maggie said.

"Jaime, I'm putting you on speaker so Sister Maggie can ask you something."

"Sister Maggie leaned in closer to the microphone. "Jaime, do you blame your cousin for nearly getting you killed?"

"No, of course not. First of all, Casey never twisted my arm—" he laughed at his own unintended pun. "But seriously, I was game from the get-go, and I was the one driving. So, I have to apologize for almost getting *you* killed, Casey. What did the doctor say about the concussion?

"I'm okay," she replied. "Are you in a lot of pain?"

"I've got pills for that," Jaime said with a peppy voice. "Sister Rose Marie convinced me to spend a few days at your convent. I can't wait to see Courtney."

"Courtney loves to cuddle, doesn't she, Sister Mary Felicia?" Sister Maggie added. "She tends to wander out of your room and into mine at night. Last night she ended up sleeping on my bed."

"Courtney?" Sister Mary Felicia looked confused.

"Yes, Courtney, the kitten you rescued, dear."

"Oh, yes, sorry, I'm a little fuzzy-brained, I guess."

"I'm sure it will pass," Jaime said. "You need sleep."

"Exactly," Sister Maggie added. "And I'm sure between home-cooked meals at the convent and a few days in bed, you'll both feel better."

"See you at the convent, Casey. I bet they'll release you tomorrow." Jaime gave a loud yawn over the phone. "Take care."

"See you later." Sister Maggie clicked off and slipped the phone back in her pocket.

"I don't think I'll ever feel better."

"What do you mean?" Sister Maggie asked.

"My poor choices always end up getting people killed." Sister Mary Felicia's eyes seemed to glaze over as though she were staring at something far away. Was she reliving that other car crash that had led to the tragedy of losing her little brother Joshua?

Sister Maggie snapped her fingers in front of Sister Mary Felicia. "Do you know where you are?"

Sister Mary Felicia continued to stare straight ahead. It was as though she'd become trapped in the past.

"Can you tell me what city we're in?" Sister Maggie asked as she waved her hand in front of the young nun's face.

Sister Mary Felicia took a breath as though she'd been holding it. Finally, she turned to Sister Maggie. "Indianapolis. I'm in Indianapolis."

Sister Maggie sighed with relief. "You need to rest tonight. And the nurse will be checking on you every fifteen minutes. Everything will be fine. I promise," she said reassuringly.

"Sister Maggie, I don't know what I'd do without you."

"Well, you don't have to worry about that I'll be sticking around to boss you a bit more. Now, close your eyes and rest while I pray

Vespers out loud. Then, I'll get us a couple of burgers from the cafeteria."

Sister Mary Felicia closed her eyes and was fast asleep before Sister Maggie had even begun the Evening Prayer of the Church. Sister Maggie was worried. She buzzed for the nurse so she could tell her what happened. She hoped the young woman's memory lapse had nothing to do with her concussion. Then again, if it had to do with re-opening wounds from her past emotional trauma, it would be just as challenging for Sister Mary Felicia to overcome.

CHAPTER FOURTEEN

May 2, 3:30 p.m.
Woodbury Animal Clinic
Indianapolis, Indiana

"Dale says Courtney is doing well. Why don't we leave her here for a bit while you and Sister Mary Felicia come by my house for coffee? Then on your way back to the convent, you can pick up your sweet kitten."

"We don't want to interfere with your plans," Sister Maggie said.

"I left work early today and only dropped by to see Dale for a minute. By sheer luck, I ran into your follow-up appointment."

"That's a lovely offer," said Sister Maggie. "I could use some caffeine right about now. How about you, Sister Mary Felicia?"

"Sounds good to me." The young nun responded as she unconsciously touched her forehead above her right eyebrow. Her scar from the car crash was healing and the swelling was gone.

"You can follow me. The house is only a few minutes away from the clinic." Charlie turned to Sister Mary Felicia. "Have the two men in the pickup truck been arrested yet?"

"Arrested and already out on bail," complained Sister Mary Felicia.

"Well, they haven't gotten away with anything yet," Sister Maggie added. "They haven't set a court date, but Mitch Fowler and Dylan King have hefty charges over their heads, including reckless driving, driving under the influence, and drug possession with the attempt to sell. Even Frank King was arrested for brandishing an illegal firearm at police as his son and Fowler were taken into custody. The police obtained a warrant to search the King Cleaning Supply warehouse for illegal firearms and other contraband," Sister Maggie said.

"Thankfully, you and Jaime are both okay," Charlie said as they headed to their cars.

A few minutes later, they arrived at a ranch-style house on a large property bordered by a white picket fence. The front yard boasted beautifully trimmed topiaries and majestic red maple trees. Charlie opened the front door, and two golden retrievers greeted them with rubber toys in their mouths and tails thumping on the floor.

"Meet Horatio and Harry," said Charlie with a chuckle as she patted the dogs on their heads. "Always ready for playtime."

The dogs dropped their toys to the ground and began sniffing at the tunics of both nuns.

"Y'all go easy on my guests," said Charlie. "It doesn't look like y'all are afraid of dogs."

"Oh, I love animals. I grew up on a farm with pigs, goats, horses, dogs, and cats," said Sister Mary Felicia, as she crouched down and began to pet the tail-wagging duo.

"When I was growing up, we had a poodle who thought she was human," added Sister Maggie. "Her name was Precious, and she never let us forget it." They all laughed.

Charlie led the sisters to a formal living room. "Coffee and cake coming up."

The living room was furnished in a contemporary design with charcoal gray walls and a beige leather sectional with bright red cushions adding pops of color. "Make yourselves at home," Charlie said. "I'll just get the coffee going."

Sister Maggie noted the wall-to-wall gun cabinets at the other end of the long room and strolled over to look at them. Sister Mary Felicia trailed behind her.

"Dale wasn't kidding when he said his father was a gun aficionado," Sister Maggie said.

One horizontal cabinet mounted on the wall held guns and rifles that looked like they belonged in a Wild West museum. A small brass plaque read "1783-1920."

"Sister Maggie, I don't think that's a good idea," Sister Mary Felicia said as Sister Maggie reached for the handle of one of the display cabinets.

"I'm just curious to have a look at these. My Dad would have loved to handle them," Sister Maggie added.

"Charlie said we could make ourselves comfortable, but I'm sure she didn't mean start snooping in her husband's gun collection," Sister Mary Felicia cautioned. "Besides, Charlie will be back any minute now."

"Well, the glass doors all seem to be locked in any case."

Within moments Charlie reappeared in the living room with a rolling cart and Horatio and Harry in tow. "Watch out, these two fellas might steal a piece of cake from your plate. Which is why we have absolutely no chocolate in the house."

"Smart idea, although I don't think I could manage to get through two days in a row without chocolate," Sister Maggie said jokingly as they made their way back to the sectional.

"I see you noticed that big 'ol gun collection." Charlie rolled her eyes. "Most people stand with mouths agape when they see it for the first time. Personally, I detest the display and think it belongs in a museum."

"It looks quite valuable," Sister Mary Felicia said. "I bet there are a lot of museums that would love to house it for historical value alone."

"I agree," Charlie said as she poured them each a cup of the steaming brew. "But when I brought it up in the past, Dale told me emphatically he wasn't ready to part with them. Who knows why?"

Charlie sliced three thick pieces of the coffee cake and handed Sister Maggie and Sister Mary Felicia each a plate.

"Mm. This is delicious," Sister Maggie said after taking a bite.

"Thank you, it's homemade cinnamon crumble coffee cake. I make up several batches and freeze them for when we have company. I'll send you home with a loaf."

"Thank you," Sister Maggie said. "I'm sure Sister Ruthie would love the recipe as well.

"I'll email it to you," Charlie said with a smile.

Sister Maggie made short work of the coffee cake and turned her attention to a dog-eared book on the coffee table. "Mind if I look at this?" she asked.

"Of course not. You're the only guest who's ever shown an interest in it. It belonged to Dale's dad, and Dale keeps it out so he can flip through it every once in a while."

The book held a history of weaponry up to 1950, and the paper dust jacket was frayed and ripped. "It's in terrible shape, but he wants it exactly as it is. The way his father kept it."

Sister Maggie turned the pages gently. "I think I can understand why. It's an excellent resource—even includes information about the ammo used for each firearm, bow, or cannon."

"If you'd like to borrow it, I'm sure Dale wouldn't mind," Charlie said.

Sister Maggie nodded. "I will take you up on that. I won't keep it more than a week, and I'll return it promptly. Unchanged, of course."

Sister Maggie thought of the mischievous kitten and considered placing the book in a bag in her closet away from Courtney's curious paws.

"How did you and Dale meet?" asked Sister Mary Felicia as she poured cream into her coffee.

"We met on a blind date when I was based in New York City. My friend and co-worker Lisa introduced us. She knew Dale from veterinary school and thought we'd be compatible. Lisa, her fiancé Marcus, Dale, and I went out for dinner one night. I was working with the orangutans at the New York State Zoo at the time. The zoo had an opening for a wildlife vet there, and both Lisa and I brought it up and encouraged Dale to apply. He aced the interview and got the job.

Working at the same place, we really got to know each other. We began dating, and within months we were engaged. I told Lisa she should go into business as a matchmaker," Charlie said.

"Were you and Dale at the New York State Zoo when Sam arrived from Borneo with baby Leo?" asked Sister Maggie.

Charlie nodded. "I'm the one who taught Sam sign language. My younger brother, Justin, is deaf. I'm from a rural area outside Montgomery, Alabama, so it was important for the whole family to be able to communicate with Justin. I even taught sign language to some of his friends. Anyway, Sam and I were given the green light to start teaching Leo modified ASL."

"What made you and Dale leave the New York State Zoo?" asked Sister Mary Felicia as she poured herself a second cup of coffee.

Charlie patted Horatio, who'd plopped down beside her. "Dale was the first to leave. He said he preferred working as a vet with domestic animals. He found out the owner of the practice here was retiring, and he bought it from him."

"Had you secured your job at the Indiana State Zoo before you left New York?" Sister Maggie asked.

"Eventually. My boss at the New York Zoo and Dr. Bob Souter are good friends," Charlie replied. "Bob wanted to bring in orangutans and other primates for his zoo, and it turned out to be a perfect fit for me. Both Dale and I love Indianapolis. New York is great, but we both prefer living in a smaller city."

"I love it too," Sister Mary Felicia said. "I'm from a small, rural town as well. How long have you and Dale been married?"

"Four years." Charlie refilled her cup and added cream and sugar.

Sister Maggie sensed there was something more Charlie wanted to share as she noted the pensive look on the young woman's face as she stirred her coffee.

"We both wanted to start a family. That was one of the reasons we decided to move here, but I couldn't conceive. We went for medical tests to determine the problem, but they had no answers for us. We even began to look into foreign adoption. Then we got the big surprise. I found out in March that I'm pregnant."

"Congratulations," Sister Mary Felicia said. "What a blessing."

"Yes, we're both thrilled. I am so ready to be a mom," Charlie said as she stood up. "The baby bump is beginning to show," she said as she pulled her uniform shorts over her almost flat belly.

"That's what my stomach looks like after a holiday meal," joked Sister Maggie. Then, she added with a serious tone, "Sometimes, God delays the gift of life only to surprise you at a later time."

Charlie sat back down, her eyes bright with tears. Sister Mary Felicia leaned forward and patted Charlie's hand.

"This may shock you," Charlie said. "But Dale and I had discussed getting a divorce a few months ago before I found out I was pregnant."

"I'm sorry to hear that," Sister Maggie said.

"I wanted a baby so badly, but Dale was focused on work, putting in sixty or more hours a week."

"But you decided to stay together," Sister Mary Felicia added. "And, now you have concrete evidence of your love for each other in this new life within you."

Charlie's hand went to her abdomen again. "This baby is a pure gift from God." She paused. "Initially, Dale questioned if it was his."

Shocked to hear Charlie's words, Sister Maggie straightened up. "Why would he say such a thing?"

Charlie looked away. "Dale can be jealous at times. The reason he left the New York Zoo wasn't only to start his own vet practice. He and I broke up for a while. After Sam came on board in New York with Leo at the zoo, I spent a lot of time teaching him how to sign. We became good friends. Dale got jealous. He didn't believe I was serious about a future with him because of my friendship with Sam. He broke off our engagement and moved to Indiana earlier than he'd intended," Charlie said, tears flowing down her cheeks.

"That must have been a difficult time for you," Sister Maggie said, handing Charlie a tissue from the box.

"I began to fall apart because I've always loved Dale," she said, dabbing at her eyes. "After he broke our engagement, I felt so abandoned and alone. Sam and I became closer. He told me about his own experiences in Indianapolis and what happened to him in college.

Sam still had the scars from that. One thing led to another, and Sam and I sought each other for comfort."

"But then you reconciled with Dale?" Sister Mary Felicia asked.

"Yes, but it was a rocky road. I didn't want to start our marriage off with any murkiness or misunderstandings, so I admitted the truth to Dale—that I'd had a brief affair with Sam at the time we'd broken up. Ironic, isn't it? Dale accused me of cheating on him with Sam and broke up with me for no reason. Then after he leaves me, I end up turning to Sam." She shook her head. "Dale and I worked through it. I started going to church again, and I even went to confession. I wanted to wipe the slate clean," Charlie added.

Sisters Maggie and Mary Felicia nodded with understanding. Charlie's humility spoke volumes of her need to show her remorse for a past lapse in judgment and her desire to heal any rift with her husband.

"To be a Christian means to forgive the inexcusable because God has forgiven the inexcusable in you," Sister Maggie said, quoting C.S. Lewis.

"Thank you both for listening to me," Charlie said, reaching for their hands. "It felt good to get that out."

"When we share our burdens, it can help us to heal," Sister Maggie said. She remembered what Father O'Connor had said about Dale Junior walking out on his father on the man's deathbed. But people can change, and perhaps Charlie had inspired Dale to change, especially with the baby on the way. She hoped so.

CHAPTER FIFTEEN

May 2, 11 p.m.
Our Lady of Guadalupe Convent
New Hope, Indiana

SISTER MAGGIE TOSSED and turned in bed and finally sat up. She turned on her bed lamp and reached for the antique gun book Charlie had lent her. Sister Maggie hadn't had much luck online with her research. Sometimes a book was still the best source of information. She flipped through the pages, perusing the pictures of antique bullets and guns, looking for the bullet she'd seen in her vision.

"Bingo!"

It was the same type of bullet Sam had shown her in her dream. "It has to be it." It was brass colored, long and pointed, and looked nothing like most bullets used in modern guns. Sister Maggie ran her finger around the image of the bullet. It was featured in a photograph next to a Remington revolver with a mother-of-pearl grip.

She recalled the various antique firearms displayed in Dale's cabinets. After speaking with Father O'Connor about Dale's relationship with his father and then hearing Charlie's story, Sister Maggie couldn't help but wonder about Dale and his antique gun collection.

But there had been no Remington revolvers on display, and none of the guns had mother-of-pearl grips. All the guns and rifles in the cabinets had brass plates engraved with the names of the firearms and the year the gun was first manufactured. But the oldest firearms were from 1783-1920. The display contained no empty holsters, either.

Could Mitch Fowler or Dylan King be antique gun collectors as well? Jose had mentioned Frank King had run out of the warehouse waving an antique firearm at the police.

Some of those old firearms are certainly worth a lot. They might have bought a stash of old guns from a seller who had no idea of their worth. Could they have used one of the antique guns to kill Sam, knowing they were going to unload it to a foreign buyer, perhaps?

Sister Maggie decided to call Jose Torres again in the morning. He might have an update on the contraband found at the warehouse.

Putting the book back on her night table, Sister Maggie slid under the covers, closed her eyes, and turned onto her side facing the door. When she opened her eyes, she spied a pair of green eyes staring at her from the doorway.

"Courtney, what you are doing out there? Come, Sweetie," she said as she patted the bed.

The little kitten didn't move. Perhaps she wanted to be picked up and put in bed. Her spaying may have caused some discomfort.

"Okay, little one," said Sister Maggie as she got out of bed.

As soon as she bent down to pick up Courtney, the kitten took off in the direction of Sister Mary Felicia's room.

"You're a fickle little kitty," Sister Maggie said. She turned around to return to her bed, but she heard an unusual sound down the long hallway. It sounded like someone moaning. Fearing one of the sisters was ill, she put on her slippers and grabbed her robe, then made her way down the hallway. Another groan reached her ears. It was coming from the guest room.

Odd.

The door was closed. They usually kept the guest room door open if they didn't have guests. No one was staying in the upstairs room. The downstairs guestroom was for male visitors or relatives only. It was where Jaime had recuperated for the first few days after the car crash.

Sister Maggie opened the door and stepped inside. But rather than seeing the bed and side table, she found herself back in the coroner's lab.

This time, the gurney where Sam's body had been was empty. She turned around to leave when a groan suddenly came from behind her. She spun around and saw Sam, fully dressed in his zookeeper outfit. The hole from the gunshot wound to his head was clearly visible.

"Sam, I've narrowed down your killer to Mitch Fowler, Dylan King, or Frank King. And there's someone else, but I just can't see him capable of murder."

Sam kept staring at her.

"Which one?" she asked. "One of them murdered you,"

Sam shook his head.

"I don't understand, Sam. One of them killed you," she protested. "Why won't you tell me which one?"

Sam shook his head again.

"Another riddle? I'm supposed to decipher it?"

Sam pointed to his gunshot wound again.

"You know, I'm getting tired of these supposed rules you folks have on the other side. Simplicity is a virtue on this side of eternity. It should be the same on your side. Why not just reveal who killed you?"

Sam began to take a few steps back and then seemed to dissolve into the shadows.

"Sam… Sam…" Sister Maggie called out.

Sister Maggie gasped and opened her eyes. She was no longer in the coroner's lab but back in bed with Courtney curled up at her feet.

"I'm glad at least one of us is asleep," she muttered.

Sister Maggie took out her red-leather journal from her night table. She dated the page and wrote *Sam appeared to me again in a dream back in the coroner's lab.*

When I asked him if one of the AHN members pulled the trigger he shook his head.

I don't understand.

Maybe Jose Torres can shed some light on the antique weapon that killed Sam.

Sister Maggie sighed and slipped the journal back into her bedside table. Her supernatural dreams always left her drained. She lay back in bed and closed her eyes, allowing sleep to take hold.

* * *

A DRIP of water landed on her head. And then another. And another. She opened her eyes and found herself in a tunnel with barely any light to see by.

Another clue from Sam? I wish he would just show me what I need to know.

A flash of light blinded her, and Sister Maggie covered her eyes. When she opened them, she saw Catie standing a few feet away. Her beautiful red hair hung damp around her shoulders, and covered in debris. She wore the same navy shorts and blue-and-white striped tank top she had on when she'd disappeared all those years ago, but they seemed to be caked in mud. She had no sneakers on her feet.

"Catie…Catie…Who did this to you?"

Catie stood against the stone wall of the tunnel.

"I looked into ARS Industrial Supplies. They have satellite offices across the country and sell their supplies from coast to coast. I'm at a loss to figure out if the person who killed you worked for ARS or still does."

Catie nodded and took a step closer to Sister Maggie.

"ARS is owned by the Stanley family. Did Ray Stanley kill you?"

Catie shook her head.

"Did your kidnapper work for ARS?"

Catie nodded.

"Did he have a white T-shirt with the word "COACH" on it? probed Sister Maggie.

Another nod. Catie gestured for Sister Maggie to turn around. Another flash of light blinded Sister Maggie, and a pile of stones fell at her feet. Some were large, and others were small, as though an explosion had caused them to break up and land in such a way.

Sister Maggie felt an electrical jolt surge through her body and her eyes flew open.

She was back in bed once more. With a deep sigh, she reached for her journal again and wrote down what she had received from Catie. She closed her eyes and tried to see all the details in the tunnel where she'd seen her sister. She even tried to sketch the mound of stones that had landed around her feet.

She tried to remember where and when she had seen that tunnel, if ever. She had no memory of it. She wondered if it was near the amusement park.

Could Catie's killer have left her body in that tunnel? If so, how had the police missed it all those years ago?

CHAPTER SIXTEEN

May 3, 8:00 a.m.
Our Lady of Guadalupe Convent
New Hope, Indiana

"Who are you calling?" asked Sister Mary Felicia as she sat down at the kitchen table with a bowl of steaming oatmeal.

"ARS Industrial Cleaning Supplies. I've been on hold for ten minutes listening to the most annoying music. They say my call is important to them," Sister Maggie said, rolling her eyes.

"Why are you calling a cleaning supply company?" Sister Rose Marie asked as she took an apple from the fruit bowl on the breakfast table.

"Just gathering information," replied Sister Maggie.

"Sister Maggie is always gathering information about something," Sister Ruthie said as she set a plate of steaming cinnamon rolls fresh from the oven on the table.

"If we don't gather information, how are we supposed to gain knowledge?" Sister Maggie quipped, grabbing a roll. "Mm, you've outdone yourself, Sister Ruthie."

Sister Ruthie smiled at the compliment. "Thank you, Sister Maggie. I added some chopped dried apricots this time."

"Delicious." Sister Maggie stood and grabbed an extra roll for good measure.

"You should make a batch for the next bake sale," Sister Rose Marie said. "It's just around the corner."

"You're organizing that one, aren't you, Sister Mary Felicia?" Sister Maggie asked.

"Oh, yes, I am. I better add the cinnamon rolls to the list."

"Good girl. Now, if you'll excuse me, I'll be in the study if you need me." Sister Maggie made her escape as the trio of nuns got onto the subject of the upcoming bake sale. She rarely spoke about her dreams or visions to anyone unless she trusted them to understand. The special gift that had been given to her as an adolescent was something she accepted willingly since it often helped the deceased find closure to their lives as they transitioned to eternity.

The first time she'd experienced the ability to see beyond what most people perceive through their five senses occurred after the tragic loss of Catie at the amusement park in Miami, some five decades before. At the time, thirteen-year-old Maureen had watched her grieving parents try to cope with the reality that her twin had been kidnapped and killed. Even more agonizing for the family was they could never have closure because Catie's body was never recovered.

She'd had her first fleeting vision of Catie days after she'd gone missing from the amusement park during a family vacation. The Donovans had planned the trip for months with their friends the Amato family. Josie Amato was best friends with Maureen and Catie. After the kidnapping, the Amatos returned back home and the Donovans stayed for several weeks as the police investigated. Maureen's dad, John Sr. a captain in the NYPD at the time, had been involved in the investigation as well. Maureen had had the vision in the hotel where they were staying, after Catie's disappearance. Her sister had appeared to her for a few seconds after Maureen had gone to the bathroom in the middle of the night. She didn't tell her parents at the time because she was too scared and distraught. Then six months later, back home, Maureen awoke one night and saw Catie standing at the foot of the bed in the bedroom they shared. Catie was holding her arms tightly against her chest as though she were a mummy.

"Catie?" Maureen had cried out several times and leaped up to touch her. At that very instant, her twin disappeared. Maureen wasn't sure if it had been a dream or a vision. When her parents ran into the bedroom, Maureen told them Catie had appeared to her. Her father shook his head, grumbled that it was just a bad dream, and went back to bed.

Her mother, on the other hand, understood what Maureen had seen, but she told her it was best not to mention it to John Senior. "Your dad doesn't believe in anything other than hard physical evidence," Lulu had said. "If you ever see Catie again when you're awake, or even if you dream about her, you can come to me and we can talk about it."

The rest of that night, Lulu had sat in bed with Maureen and held her until their tears had been spent.

Sister Maggie had begun having other visions after that, visions she couldn't explain to herself let alone others. But none were of Catie. She talked about them with Lulu, and then after she joined the Adorers of Divine Love she confided in Father O'Connor and Mother Superior, Sister Marie Claire. And over the years, Sister Maggie had also learned how to interpret the visions as a way to help the families and friends of the deceased. Then, after so many decades had passed, Sister Maggie began having visions of Catie again. And to Sister Maggie, that meant something. It meant that perhaps they could finally find Catie and bring her home.

Although Sister Maggie would never describe herself as clairvoyant, she did acknowledge she could grasp realities beyond normal sensory experiences. Raised a devout Catholic, Sister Maggie was taught that the dead weren't to be contacted for information or favors, and the future was unconditionally in God's providential care.

Over the years, she'd crossed paths with several charlatans who claimed to be psychic but whose primary motive was greed and taking advantage of people grieving the loss of a loved one.

"ARS Industrial Cleaning Supplies. May I help you?"

Sister Maggie set down the half-eaten cinnamon roll and sat forward in her office chair. "I certainly hope you can help me. I'm looking for the names of the salesmen who worked for your company in the state of Florida some forty-five to fifty years ago. I know this is an unusual request."

"Ma'am, this is not information we give out to the general public. Your name?"

"My name is Sister Margaret Mary Donovan."

"Sister Maggie, is that you?" The woman's voice said on the other side of the line. "This is Melissa Mendez. My maiden name was Gonzalez. Do you remember me? I was in your parish youth group at St. Malachy Parish in Brooklyn."

Sister Maggie exclaimed, "Mel, of course, I remember you, my dear. What are you doing in Florida? We lost touch with your family after you moved upstate."

"We moved a few times. Living upstate was too expensive, and my dad was worried about the crime rate in Brooklyn at the time. So, he decided to move us to Florida, where he opened a coffee shop. Eventually, I went to college here, married my wonderful husband, Gustavo Mendez, and we have three beautiful daughters."

"What a wonderful blessing, indeed." Melissa, or Mel, as she was called, was of Puerto Rican heritage. The mix of Spanish, African, and indigenous Taíno and Carib-Indian ethnicities accounted for Mel's unique beauty as a girl. Sister Maggie knew the former beauty pageant winner was just as beautiful inside.

"I'm so happy to hear that things turned out well for your family," Sister Maggie said.

"Have you spoken to Father O'Connor recently? How's he doing?" Mel asked.

"I spoke to him the other day. He's doing great and still active at the parish. He just celebrated his eighty-third birthday."

"That's wonderful. I send him a Christmas card every year. I'll have to call him and tell him we spoke," said Mel. She paused. "Sister Maggie, the information you requested is not given out because of privacy issues. However, since I'm also the office manager here, and because it's you, I will make an exception."

"It has to do with my twin sister's disappearance more than fifty years ago."

"I remember my parents telling my siblings and me about it when we first moved here. They were overprotective of us."

"I'm glad they told you and watched over you, Serena, and your brother Diego. Yes, Catie's disappearance is a cold case, but through the years, I have discovered certain facts that might help me get the case reopened. I recently found out my sister may have had contact with an employee from ARS Industrial Cleaning Supplies in Florida the day she disappeared. It might make him a person of interest in the case," Sister Maggie said as she took a pad and pen from the drawer.

"How did you find this out?" asked Mel.

"It's a long story," Sister Maggie replied. The last thing she wanted to do was try to explain to Mel her vision of Catie pointing to the ARS soap dispenser in the restroom at the Indiana State Zoo. "Can you help me? I need to review a list of male ARS employees in Florida between the ages of eighteen and thirty who worked for the company forty-five to fifty-five years ago."

"Well, what I can tell you is that the Florida employees were few in number that many years ago. I'm actually looking at a map on the wall that shows how the Stanley company expanded its sales through the years. You may not know this, but the company started selling its supplies in Brooklyn in the 1950s, mostly to schools. According to the map, the company set up a satellite office in Florida by the 1990s. Before that date, they had a handful of salesmen going to schools, office buildings, and other sites that had public restrooms. Can you give me a few days to dig a bit deeper?"

Sister Maggie could barely contain her excitement. "Of course, Mel. I can't tell you how much this means to me." Sister Maggie gave Mel her mobile phone number and her email address.

"What a coincidence you reached me and not someone else here at the office. I hope I can help you and your family find closure to Catie's tragic disappearance," said Mel.

"My talking to you today was no coincidence—it was God's providence," Sister Maggie replied.

CHAPTER SEVENTEEN

May 4, 7:00 p.m.
Our Lady of Guadalupe Convent
New Hope, Indiana

"SNOID IS an adorable beagle and so friendly," Sister Mary Felicia said as she held Courtney against her chest while at the same time carefully bending down to pet the dog. Sister Maggie grinned at the adorable little dog. Jaime had called earlier to say he would be stopping by with a surprise. *And what a lovely surprise,* Sister Maggie thought.

"His former owners told me his name is Mr. Snoid III. He answers to Mr. Snoid," said Jaime. "Charlie Wells knew I was looking for a dog after I spent a week at your convent with the kitten as company. My apartment is pet friendly, and it seemed so empty without a companion, so I thought of giving a rescue dog a good life."

"What a wonderful idea," Sister Maggie said.

"Why would his owners give up this sweet little boy? How old is he?" Sister Mary Felicia asked as Courtney became curious about the other four-legged creature.

"Mr. Snoid is about eight years old. The owner told me her

daughter was about to give birth in California and needed her help. Her daughter and son-in-law invited her to stay with them in their two-bedroom apartment building. Not only is that a tight space, but management also prohibits pets. Mrs. Eaton asked Charlie to find Mr. Snoid a permanent home. I promised her I would send photos of Mr. Snoid to her in the future," explained Jaime.

Courtney leaped out of Sister Mary Felicia's arms. The kitten immediately faced Mr. Snoid, who stepped away from her and positioned himself behind Jaime. Sister Maggie noticed the kitten's rear end begin to wiggle—a sure sign she was in a playful mood and ready to pounce. Sister Maggie immediately scooped up Courtney and held her. "Let's not cause trouble for our new little friend," Sister Maggie cautioned. She sat with the kitten on the oversized armchair in the community room. Jaime and Sister Mary Felicia and Mr. Snoid sat on the sofa.

"How's the arm doing?" Sister Mary Felicia asked Jaime.

"No surgery needed. In a few weeks, I'll get this cast-off."

Sister Mary Felicia looked relieved.

"And your head?" asked Jaime.

"Unfortunately, the headaches are frequent," Sister Mary Felicia replied. "Have you heard anything about the warehouse criminals?"

"No. Nothing," replied Jaime.

Sister Maggie handed Courtney to Sister Mary Felicia as her cell phone rang. "It's Jose Torres. Watch her. She has that mischievous look in those green eyes."

Sister Mary Felicia laughed. "I'll be careful she doesn't intimidate Mr. Snoid."

Sister Maggie put Jose Torres on speaker so Jaime and Sister Mary Felicia could follow the conversation.

Sister Mary Felicia yelled out, "I hear the Kings and Fowler are out on bail!"

Sister Maggie put her index finger to her mouth and asked, "Do you have any updates on the ballistics report for the murder weapon?" Sister Maggie asked.

"The fatal bullet came from an antique Remington revolver made during the early twentieth century," Jose replied.

"Did you find any such revolvers at King Cleaning Supplies?" Sister Maggie asked.

"You're one step ahead of me, Sister Maggie," Jose said.

"Sister Maggie is one step ahead of everyone," added Jaime.

"In addition to modern firearms, we discovered bomb components. We found a trap door in the floor that went down to what looked like a small cellar. They kept cleaning supplies in it, but the police also discovered a door leading to a tunnel—quite a long one. At the end of the tunnel was an underground bunker, and that's where our team uncovered all sorts of goodies, including a cache of antique firearms."

Sister Maggie couldn't help but remember her dream about Catie in the tunnel. They couldn't be related, could they?

"We uncovered several Remington revolvers including one with a mother-of-pearl handle. The weapon had been fired in the recent past. The bullet that killed Sam came from that revolver," said Jose.

"So, Frank King was selling modern firearms and antique weapons on the side," Sister Maggie said.

"Quite an entrepreneur," Jaime added.

"No wonder he chased us out of there that day and then had his son and bosom buddy run us off the highway," Sister Mary Felicia said.

"Appears so. There's a black market for all kinds of contraband in this country," added Jose.

"The fact that you found the murder weapon at King's Warehouse and that Dylan had had a public altercation with Sam the day before the murder—wouldn't that be enough to make the case stick?" Jaime asked.

"Frank and Dylan King, and Mitch Fowler are facing significant prison time on the current charges," Sister Maggie said. "Could a deal be made that would encourage one of them to sing?"

"I suspect they will all be tight-lipped right now," Jose replied. "I could talk to the prosecutor, Laura Wilson, about trying to get one of them to turn on the other two. The most likely turncoat would be Mitch Fowler. He has a major drug problem and appears to be the weakest link."

"Do you think the AHN put a hit on Sam because he was a defector?" Sister Maggie asked. "The main reason he stayed out of Indiana all those years was because the AHN had threatened him after he had to recuse himself in one of their trials."

"But after all those years?" Jaime asked. "The AHN could have gotten rid of Sam back then during the trial. But they didn't. Besides, Sam abandoned the legal profession and left for Borneo to work with animals and conservation. Even when he came back to the States, he went to work at the New York State Zoo before he came to Indiana."

"Exactly," Jose added. "Why kill a guy who threw away his career as a lawyer to work with monkeys?"

Rather than correct her friend and tell him Sam had worked with apes, Sister Maggie replied, "Thank you, Jose. Let us know how things progress."

"Anything for you, Sister Maggie," Jose said. "Sister Mary Felicia and Jaime, did you know that Sister Maggie helped me bring down one of the worst drug dealers in Brooklyn many years back?"

"We had no idea," Sister Mary Felicia said.

"The drug dealer was Enrique Morales, who was also my cousin—broke my mother's heart that her late sister's son had fallen so low. I wasn't officially on the case because of my relationship with Enrique. But one of the detectives got a tip that my cousin intended to kidnap my boy, Angel, from St. Malachy School. It was part of a plot to get me to intervene on Enrique's behalf and get the charges dropped. Thank God, Sister Maggie was there to protect Angel," Jose said, his voice cracking with emotion.

Sister Maggie closed her eyes and remembered that day when Jose had made a frantic call to her at the parish office just fifteen minutes before the school day finished. She'd hung up the phone and ran to Angel's first-grade class as they lined up at the door. She took his teacher aside, Sister Theresa, and told her Angel was in danger and she needed to stall taking her class into the schoolyard.

Sister Maggie pulled Angel out of the line and told him they were going to run a race to the convent car to hide as part of a game. Angel nodded in excitement as Sister Theresa encouraged him. They made it down the first-floor hallway and exited the back door of the school to the parking lot behind the rectory, where she hid Angel in the back seat of her car and covered him with a blanket. She told him to stay put and to be absolutely silent no matter what he heard outside. It was part of the game.

"I never knew exactly what transpired between you and Enrique that day," Jose said.

"After I hid your son in the car, I went to the schoolyard where Sister Theresa was just leading the kids out. The children were organized into a double line. The parents began arriving to pick up their children. Sister Theresa took your wife Marisol to the principal's office and explained the situation while I handled her class."

Sister Maggie took a deep breath and continued. "Enrique approached, and his eyes darted around the schoolyard, clearly looking for Angel. That's when I gestured to him and asked if he needed any assistance. He said he was there on behalf of Jose Torres, his cousin. He said that you'd asked him to pick up Angel because of a family emergency. I told him they must have gotten their wires crossed because Angel had already been picked up by his grandmother.

"Of course, Enrique must have become agitated," Jose added. "I'm sure he was packing heat as well."

"I went into my dry and dull administrator mode," Sister Maggie said. "Hoping it would keep things on a placid level. I calmly began to run through our school rules when it comes to picking up children. I stated that a family member who was not a parent or legal guardian needed prior written permission. And I was happy to bring him into the principal's office to fill out the necessary paperwork for next time. I kept him there for as long as I could as I went through all the school's regulations. By that time, the police sirens could be heard. Enrique took off running and cursing his head off," Sister Maggie said.

"I am eternally grateful to you for keeping my son safe," Jose said. "I will do my best to work with local authorities and find Sam Browning's murderer," insisted Jose.

"I have faith in you, Jose," Sister Maggie said. "By the way, how is Angel doing these days?"

"He's an orthopedic surgeon at Johns Hopkins," replied Jose. "Marisol and I are so proud of him."

"Wonderful."

"He's kept up with his running," Jose added. "I think your mad dash out of the school turned him into a life-long runner."

"Well, it had the opposite effect on me. My feet couldn't take it," Sister Maggie said as she looked down at her aching feet.

CHAPTER EIGHTEEN

May 5, 11:00 a.m.
Our Lady of Guadalupe Convent
New Hope, Indiana

"JAIME TOLD me Leo is still asking for Sam, but a new zookeeper named Travis Campbell has piqued his interest," Sister Mary Felicia said as she stepped into the office at the convent.

"Well, that's good to know," Sister Maggie said, putting away the file she was working on.

"Yes, I'm glad about it," Sister Mary Felicia said. "Travis will be working with Charlie on the interspecies communications between orangutans and humans that the Indiana State Zoo is spearheading. Dr. Souter was impressed with Travis's resumé, especially since he's also fluent in ASL. Jaime told me Leo had warmed up to Travis after he secretly and successfully slipped him a meat-cheese-bread the other day.

Sister Maggie smiled. "I'll look forward to seeing Leo again now that his spirits are lifting."

Sister Mary Felicia took a seat at her desk and rubbed her forehead. "I know headaches are an after-effect from a concussion, but they are wearing me out."

"You have another follow-up appointment with the doctor soon?"

"Yes. He said he wanted to see me again in two weeks after my first follow-up, but I'm not sure how he's going to have a remedy for these headaches."

Sister Maggie said. "Perhaps stress is also a contributing factor. You've been working hard on the new brochures and updating the reading material we'll be handing out at the fair. Why don't you go put your feet up in the community room? I'll let you know what we have scheduled next week when I finish making a few calls this morning. We also have a regional community meeting coming up. We'll need to deliver a report about our vocational outreach these past six months." Sister Maggie paused as he regarded Sister Mary Felicia's pale face. "In time, the headaches will simply become a bad memory," she said in a gentle voice. "After my head injury when I was attacked by TJ and his brother, Robbie, the headaches took about two months to go away."

Sister Mary Felicia nodded. "I recall you complaining of splitting headaches while you were recovering at John and Eileen's house in Queens."

"Oh, yes. Mama Lulu was with me 24/7 while I stayed with my brother and sister-law. It's a wonder my head didn't explode," Sister Maggie said.

"Well, I think I'll take your advice, close my eyes and put my feet up for a little while," Sister Mary Felicia said as she rose from her chair.

"Good decision," Sister Maggie said as her cell phone rang to the theme of the original *Star Trek* TV series, one of her favorite shows.

Sister Mary Felicia gave her a little wave as she left the office.

Sister Maggie swiped the phone. "Hello, Sister Maggie speaking."

"Sister Maggie, it's Jose, I've got some news."

"Jose, good to hear from you again so soon. I hope it's good."

"It could be. Mitch Fowler wants to sing like a canary."

"Well, you were right," Sister Maggie said. "Mitch Fowler really is the weak link in the chain."

"He said he's willing to cut a deal to testify against Frank and Dylan King. He told the prosecuting attorney, Laura Wilson, he has information about the illegal sales of firearms from the King warehouse to three known domestic terrorist cells. When he was questioned about the Remington revolver that killed Sam Browning, he said he knew who pulled the trigger, but he wanted the pot sweetened for himself in terms of a new and better deal," Jose said. "As soon as I get the details, I'll text or call you."

"Thanks, Jose. I have to tell you my gut says we'll be in for a surprise when we learn who killed Sam."

"My money is on Dylan King. Sam's recusal from the white supremacy trial came too late, and even though it helped Dylan and Mitch walked away from a murder conviction, I have a feeling the AHN wanted to make an example out of Sam. Fowler did King's bidding and probably covered up the murder. It's time for justice to be served. What Sam couldn't accomplish as a prosecuting attorney, he'll accomplish in death. And hopefully, we'll put those scoundrels away for life," Jose added.

"I hope so," Sister Maggie said.

"I have another call. I'll be in touch," Jose said.

They hung up just as Courtney came trotting into the office. She jumped up onto Sister Maggie's desk and dropped a neon yellow toy duck on her laptop.

"I can't play with you now," Sister Maggie said as she tossed the toy across the room.

Courtney immediately retrieved it, jumped back on the desk, and dropped the toy on the top of her hand.

"You're quite insistent," Sister Maggie said as she again threw the toy to the other side of the room. It made a quacking sound as it landed. Again, the black kitten retrieved it and brought it back. Sister Maggie rolled her eyes and threw the toy out into the hallway. This time Courtney didn't return. Out of curiosity, Sister Maggie followed the kitten and watched as the black ball of fur ran into the community room and dropped the yellow duck at Sister Mary Felicia's feet. When Sister Mary Felicia didn't reach down for the toy, Courtney put it in her mouth and jumped on the young nun's lap. Sister Maggie grinned and went back to her desk. That's when she noticed a message had been left on her cell phone. She punched in her code to retrieve it.

"Hello, Sister Maggie. This is Dale Wells. I have some sad news. Charlie suffered a miscarriage last night. She wanted you and Sister Mary Felicia to know. I just brought her home from the hospital. It was a boy—" There was a noticeable pause, Sister Maggie could hear the emotion in Dale's voice. "She told me she had wanted to name the boy after me if it was a boy. I plan to spend the next few days home with Charlie. I'm really worried about her. I've never seen her so depressed. If you have plans to drive into Indianapolis, we'd be grateful if you could stop by."

Sister Maggie sighed and went to the office window. Gazing out at the bright sunny day she spotted several baby rabbits hopping through the grass, following their mother to a safe location where predators were unwelcome. She marveled at the maternal instinct present in the animal kingdom.

The same everlasting Father who cares for you today will care for you tomorrow and every day. Either he will shield you from suffering or give you unfailing strength to bear it...

Sister Maggie understood too well how human nature reflected those wise words by St. Frances de Sales. Despite the decades that had passed since Catie's death, the pain and loss had never dulled in her soul.

Charlie was no doubt going through deep emotional pain, knowing she would never hold her baby boy in her arms in this life.

I need to visit Charlie and Dale.

CHAPTER NINETEEN

May 6, 10:30 a.m.
Indiana State Zoo
Indianapolis, Indiana

Sister Maggie took the exit for the Indiana State Zoo. Within ten minutes, she arrived and made her way to the administration building where Jaime had his office on the first floor. Sister Mary Felicia was resting in bed, back at the convent, and Sister Maggie had promised she'd check in on Jaime before visiting Charlie. She sighed. It seemed as though all the people she cared about were in some sort of pain. Jaime had gone to see his doctor about a pain in his neck, which had all the sisters worried. Sister Ruthie insisted Sister Maggie bring him back to the convent so they could look after him. Sister Maggie said she would ask him.

Sister Maggie could see Jaime through the glass panel on his office door. He wore a neck brace that supported his chin and encircled his neck with a strap.

When Jaime saw Sister Maggie, he immediately got up from his desk chair. His left arm was covered by a blue cast. Despite his apparent discomfort, he greeted her with a big smile.

"So, how's Casey?" Jaime asked.

"She's under the weather today. I thought it might be the effects of the concussion, but it turns out she caught a bad cold. The other sisters are giving her chicken noodle soup and hot tea. Courtney hasn't left her side all day. She just needs some downtime," Sister Maggie said reassuringly to Jaime. "You, on the other hand, look like you've been through a war. What's with the neck brace?"

"My doctor believes I'm experiencing delayed whiplash. The brace is supposed to stabilize my neck by supporting the injured muscles and ligaments. The pain in my neck has already improved a bit," he said.

"I'm sure Sister Ruthie would be disappointed to hear that," Sister Maggie said, her lips twitching.

"Why is that?" Jaime asked.

"She was looking forward to clucking over you like a mother hen."

They both laughed.

"I'm glad you're all watching over Casey," Jaime said after offering Sister Maggie a chair. "Casey blames herself for my injuries. She had me worried the day of the crash when she kept saying she was responsible for killing the people she loved," he added, easing himself into his office chair. "I didn't want to bring it up at dinner the other night. We were having such a nice time watching Courtney and Mr. Snoid get to know each other."

"I understand," Sister Maggie said with a nod. "I was worried too. That night in the hospital was rough for her. It seemed like she was caught in a time warp, reliving the car crash that killed her brother and driver," Sister Maggie said. "She's much better now and realizes the concussion knocked her for a loop. Also, shock can produce adverse effects on the mind and emotions. Thankfully, your cousin is recovering, except for those pesky headaches," Sister Maggie said. "But the doctor says those will pass as well."

Sister Maggie went on to update Jaime on the case, but she didn't mention her initial concerns about Dale. It didn't seem possible he could hurt a fly let alone commit a murder. He was such a caring vet and he clearly adored Charlie. His voice on the phone message he'd left sounded so full of emotion, Sister Maggie just couldn't fathom Dale doing anything so terrible. There was no sense worrying Jaime since he was a friend of both Charlie and Dale, especially with Charlie's miscarriage. Besides, given what Jose had told her, Fowler was ready to spill the beans on either Dylan King or Frank King. Maybe even both.

Jaime suggested they visit Leo and escorted Sister Maggie to one of the golf carts parked outside. "Our new zookeeper, Travis Campbell, is a hit with Leo," Jaime said. "And lucky for us, he's fluent in sign language. Since you'll be visiting Charlie this afternoon, you can lighten her spirits by giving her a report on the new dynamic duo."

"I can't wait to meet him," Sister Maggie replied.

They arrived at the orangutan exhibit and saw Travis signing to Leo, who was in a room encircled by thick glass. There were bales of straw around the room and several hammocks for the orangutans, but only Leo was in the glass-paneled room. Travis was signing to Leo from outside, and Leo was signing back.

"Only Sam was allowed to be in the same room with Leo. I have a feeling Travis will be able to convince Bob to allow him closer access to Leo in the future," Jaime said.

When Travis saw Jaime, he signed to Leo they were taking a break. At that point, Leo noticed Sister Maggie. He went up to the window panel and began signing again to Travis.

"What is he saying?" asked Sister Maggie.

"He wants to know where the song-woman is," Travis said. "Who is he talking about?"

Sister Maggie and Jaime laughed. "He's talking about my cousin, Sister Mary Felicia, the former Casey Bauer, a popular entertainer," Jaime said. "She sings to him whenever she comes to visit."

"He's signing again," Sister Maggie said.

Travis laughed. "He calls you the blue-woman. He asked if the blue-woman has a snack for him. Leo is very food-oriented."

Sister Maggie shook her head. "No snacks. Sorry. I'm glad to see he seems to be rebounding emotionally after losing Sam."

"He asks for Sam several times a day," Travis said. "He signs that

Papa-Sam was draped and is sleeping. Dr. Souter thinks he's beginning to understand Sam is not coming back. I don't think I can compete with Papa-Sam," he paused and added, "but Leo has made up a new name for me."

"I can't wait to hear this. Leo is good with names. He calls Bob Souter 'Stink-Man.'" Jaime said.

Travis's face blushed. "He calls me 'Big-Feet.'" He lifted his boot. "I have a size-fifteen foot. "I guess since I'm six foot six, I'd look ridiculous with anything smaller."

"He probably thinks you're his long-lost brother. You even have red hair," Jaime added with a hint of humor.

"My hair color is a hit with Leo." Travis grinned. "When we met, he told me he likes my hair," Travis said. "Hold on. He's signing again. He's very communicative today."

"What is he saying? It's like he's making a speech," Jaime said.

Travis shook his head. "He wants to know why you have a blue arm and neck collar. He thinks you look funny." Travis signed back to Leo and explained about Jaime being hurt by a car.

"What is he signing back?" Sister Maggie asked.

Travis laughed. "Leo says Jaime has a boo-boo and needs a meat-cheese-bread."

Jaime nodded. "At least he didn't ask me to get him one."

Travis added, "Leo just said *you* should get him a meat-cheese-bread."

"Leo's back to his old tricks," Jaime added.

CHAPTER TWENTY

May 6, 1:00 p.m.
Home of Dale and Charlie Wells
Indianapolis, Indiana

"CHARLIE HAS BEEN LOOKING FORWARD to seeing you."

"How are *you* doing, Dale?" Sister Maggie asked as Dale led her into the house.

"I've been better. I've been working so many long hours at the clinic since one of my vets is on maternity leave. Ironic huh? I hope I didn't miss any of the signs that Charlie's own pregnancy was in trouble," said Dale.

"I'm sure you didn't. We often don't know something is going to happen until it does." Sister Maggie followed Dale to their family room, where Charlie was curled up on the sectional. As soon as she saw Sister Maggie, she sat up.

"Thank you for coming," Charlie said, her eyes tearing up. "You were among the few who knew I was pregnant. I asked Dale to call you and Sister Mary Felicia about our loss."

Sister Maggie gave Charlie a hug before sitting beside her.

"I'll make coffee," Dale offered."

"Thank you, Dale, that would be nice," Sister Maggie said.

After Dale left the room, Sister Maggie told Charlie about her visit with Travis and Leo. It was good to see Charlie laugh. She seemed happy that Travis and Leo were getting along so well.

"I have to tell you something that Dale confessed to me last night," Charlie began. Before she could say anything more, Dale returned to the room with a tray laden with coffee and Irish soda scones. He set it on the coffee table and poured them each a cup.

"Charlie baked these last month," Dale said as he offered a plate to Sister Maggie. "We've got a freezer full of baked goods."

Suddenly, Horatio and Harry stirred from their positions near the window where they enjoyed the afternoon sun. No doubt, the smell of the scones had roused them to investigate.

"No scones for you boys," Charlie warned. She smiled, accepted a plate, and covered her two scones with strawberry jam as Horatio and Harry tried sniffing.

The two women sipped coffee and snacked on their scones. "Delicious, Charlie." Sister Maggie loved anything homemade, especially when she didn't have to make it. The warmed scones with raisins were especially fluffy. "How you remain so thin and bake so well is a mystery to me," Sister Maggie said.

Dale's pager went off. "Excuse me. I need to take this."

When Dale left the room, Sister Maggie put her cup down and leaned in closer to Charlie. "You were about to tell me something."

Charlie nodded. "Last night, Dale wanted to talk to me about his relationship with his father. I knew his father was unfaithful to his mother. What I didn't know was how much my husband hated his father. He was insistent. He said he had to tell me everything."

"Go on," Sister Maggie urged.

"Dale told me when he was a kid, he woke up one night hearing his mother crying. He ran to their bedroom and tried to console her. When he asked his mother why Daddy wasn't home, she said he was working late, and she'd just had a bad dream. She told him to go back to bed. But there were many more nights like that one. As he got older, he realized why his mother was crying and where his dad must have been."

Sister Maggie nodded in understanding, her heart going out to Dale and what he'd gone through as a boy.

"On his death bed, Dale Senior openly apologized to his mother for his cheating," Charlie continued. "She forgave him. He asked Dale for forgiveness too."

"Did he?"

"Dale said when his mother had gone to the restroom, he told his father he would never forgive him and that his father didn't deserve forgiveness. He accused his father of asking for forgiveness because he was afraid to die and be judged by God. What's worse, he told his father there were unforgivable sins in this life and the next. Then he walked out on his father and never looked back," said Charlie.

Sister Maggie raised her eyebrows. "Heartbreaking."

Charlie sat back. "That's when Dale broke down and started to weep. H-he told me he was just like his father. At first, I thought he meant he'd cheated on me. He said no, but that his sin was unforgivable. When I pleaded with him to trust me and tell me what he'd done, he started to shake and cry harder. I asked him if he had forgiven me for my sin with Sam. He nodded that he had. I told him no matter what he had done, I would forgive him unconditionally. Sister Maggie, I've never seen Dale like that—he was sobbing like a child," Charlie stressed.

Sister Maggie was just about to ask Charlie if Dale had confessed to her what it was, when he returned to the family room.

"Honey, I have to go to the clinic to help out. A local dog rescue just brought in three dogs in rough shape. Will you be okay? It'll probably take a few hours."

Sister Maggie noticed he seemed to hesitate.

"Those poor pups," Charlie said. "Go. Take care of the animals. I'll be fine. I've got Horatio, Harry, and Sister Maggie here to keep me company."

Dale thanked Sister Maggie for visiting, kissed Charlie on the forehead, and rushed out of the room. After Dale left, Sister Maggie leaned forward and said with a calming voice, "God in His mercy, always forgives a repentant sinner. The only unpardonable sins are those for which the sinner is unrepentant and seeks no forgiveness."

"I want you to know what Dale told me. He's going to need help—your help and mine."

"I'll do whatever I can for Dale. I promise," Sister Maggie said.

CHAPTER TWENTY-ONE

May 6, 7:30 p.m.
Our Lady of Guadalupe Convent
New Hope, Indiana

"I'M glad you're feeling a little better," said Sister Maggie as she handed Sister Mary Felicia a cup of hot tea with lemon.

Sister Mary Felicia glanced at the photo of Jaime that Sister Maggie had taken at the zoo.

"Thank you for checking up on Jaime. That neck brace worries me. Did he tell you anything about it? He said he went to the doctor and everything should be fine in a few days. Other than that, he refuses to tell me anything more."

"The doctor ordered imaging of his neck, and Jaime has whiplash. He's doing fine," Sister Maggie said. "I had a lovely visit with Leo and Travis today. Leo was asking about you." Sister Maggie had texted the young nun a few pics she'd taken on her phone.

Sister Mary Felicia smiled. "What do you think about the new zookeeper, Travis? He's certainly a tall redhead."

"With big feet, as noted by Leo," added Sister Maggie. "Travis is a fascinating man. He grew up in New England and taught deaf students in Maine. Several years ago, when he turned twenty-five, he decided to get a master's degree in zoology in Wisconsin. He wanted to pursue a career studying the behavior and communication skills of orangutans. When he found out Dr. Souter needed to fill Sam's position at the orangutan exhibit, Travis applied for the position and was hired the same day."

Sister Mary Felicia leaned forward from the couch, her eyes reflecting concern. "What's wrong? You keep looking at your phone."

"What do you mean?" asked Sister Maggie.

"You seem preoccupied with something or someone," remarked Sister Mary Felicia.

"I'm concerned about Charlie and Dale Wells," Sister Maggie said.

"The loss of a baby is always difficult. Hopefully, Charlie will be able to conceive again and know the joy of motherhood," Sister Mary Felicia replied.

"Hopefully," Sister Maggie said. Her cell phone vibrated. "Oh, dear, I didn't expect this. Mama Lulu wants to Skype. Excuse me while I take her call in our office."

Sister Maggie left the community room and logged into Skype. After she accepted the call, Mama Lulu's face filled the screen.

"Maureen, your brother John was right. Skyping is the way to go. He taught me how to use the app last night. Your brother, Andrew, says I need to call you more often now that I'm a whiz at this," Mama Lulu insisted.

"Thank him for his advice," Sister Maggie said as she tapped her fingers on the desk. "How are you doing, Mom?"

"Very well, thank you, dear Maureen. How are you? I hadn't heard from you in over a week," Mama Lulu said.

"I'm sorry. Forgive me," said Sister Maggie.

"The last time you asked for my forgiveness was when you were recovering from your traumatic brain injury at John and Eileen's house. You were annoyed with me because I kept waking you when I had to use the bathroom. That happens when you get old, you know."

Sister Maggie laughed. "You going to the bathroom at night didn't annoy me. It was the fact that you felt the need to wake me up and *tell* me that you were going to the bathroom each time."

"Well, I didn't want you to be alarmed if you turned over in bed and didn't see me in the twin bed next to you," replied Mama Lulu.

"Somehow, I would have figured out where you had gone." Sister Maggie raised her eyebrows. "So, what's new?"

"This Sunday, we're having a family dinner at Dennis and Linda's house. No special occasion. I told them we needed to get a good card game going after we ate," Mama Lulu said.

"That sounds like fun," Sister Maggie said absentmindedly as she thought about her conversation with Charlie.

"What is it with you today?" Mama Lulu asked. "You don't look or sound right."

"What do you mean?" Sister Maggie asked.

"Maureen, I know you. Something is wrong. I can see it in your face. I know you have something on your mind."

"Let me ask you a question, Mom. Do you believe there's a sin that is unforgivable?"

"Are you talking about Red's killer? I told you years ago I would try to forgive him. If I couldn't forgive him in this life, I'd be willing to go to purgatory for a few centuries and work on it," Mama Lulu replied.

Sister Maggie smiled. "I'm not talking about forgiving Red's killer. I guess you've answered my question. If we struggle and strive to forgive, it means we're working on forgiving," Sister Maggie said.

"Maybe you should go to confession, Maureen. You need to forgive the person who offended you," Mama Lulu cautioned.

Sister Maggie rolled her eyes. "Mom, I'm not talking about myself. Here's another question for you. Did you ever promise to keep a secret?"

Mama Lulu paused. "Years ago, I discovered my boss was having an affair with another employee. I never revealed what I had learned to his wife, who was a good friend at the time. I didn't want to help destroy their marriage."

"That must have been difficult for you."

"It was, but I couldn't hurt my friend." Mama Lulu wagged her finger at the screen. "But if someone tells you a secret and you promise not to reveal it, you are obliged to be silent. Of course, if someone tells you he's going to kill himself, you have to get the person immediate help. Maureen, I think you know all about secrets. Just do the right thing. You're no dope."

Sister Maggie shook her head. Mama Lulu had such a way with words. She thought about what Charlie had revealed to her. She closed her eyes, and a quote from Proverbs came to her mind: "Argue your case with your neighbor, and do not reveal the secret of another."

"Maureen, are you listening to me?"

"I'm sorry, Mom. I was just thinking about something I need to do."

"Okay, well, whatever it is, get it done. It's obviously bothering you."

"It is Mom. It truly is."

CHAPTER TWENTY-TWO

May 8, 12:30 p.m.
Great Eats Restaurant
Indianapolis, Indiana

"May I take your order, Sister?" the waiter asked.

"I'll have a garden salad and a sweet, iced tea," Sister Maggie said.

"Are you sure you don't want something more substantial?" Jose asked.

"I've indulged too much this week," Sister Maggie said with a smile.

Jose ordered a burger, fries, and iced tea without sugar. "I asked you to meet me so I could fill you in on Mitch Fowler and the Kings. Unfortunately, Mitch refused to tell Laura Wilson who killed Sam. They offered him a reduced sentence in a minimum-security prison far away from his former buddies in crime.

"Mitch and his lawyer countered by asking for probation and an ankle monitor," Jose added. "Laura said no way and bluffed him. She told him we were closing in on some very damning evidence."

"I suspect Fowler may try to use his knowledge of the killer at some point in the future," Sister Maggie said as she unfolded her white napkin and put it on her lap. She watched Jose as he checked emails on his phone. The years had been kind to him. His black hair remained thick and was now streaked with silver. As a young officer, he didn't wear eyeglasses. Now he sported sleek black frames that made him look like an FBI agent from a 1950s movie.

"What can you tell me about Laura Wilson, the prosecuting attorney?" asked Sister Maggie.

"I know Laura personally from when she was an ADA in Manhattan. She and Marisol are friends as well—they did a lot of charity work together. Laura is a woman of integrity. She's not about keeping a scorecard on convictions. She's meticulous about the facts that are presented to her. From what Marisol told me, Laura felt guilty after she helped to convict an innocent man of murder early on in her career, before she worked in Manhattan. It turns out he spent five years in prison. When she discovered DNA evidence that proved he was innocent, she went to him and apologized and had him exonerated. The extraordinary thing is he forgave her. That experience changed her and made her a better prosecutor," Jose said.

Sister Maggie nodded. "She sounds like an exceptional person."

"She is. Both she and Marisol are still very close friends."

"By the way, how is Marisol doing?" asked Sister Maggie.

"She's doing volunteer work for the St. Vincent de Paul Society. She's always had a heart for the poor," Jose said.

"And Dr. Angel Torres?" Sister Maggie asked.

"He's working hard as an orthopedic surgeon. Marisol keeps telling him that as an only child, he should consider getting married sooner rather than later because she wants a lot of grandchildren to spoil," Jose said.

When the food arrived, Sister Maggie and Jose said grace together. "I promised to find Sam's killer, but so far, we don't have any concrete evidence of who pulled that trigger," Jose said, adding black pepper to his fries.

Sister Maggie sipped her iced tea. Her mind traveled back to her childhood when she had promised to help Catie study over the summer so she wouldn't fall behind in math when the school term started in the fall. Math had always been Catie's weakest subject, but Maggie had always aced it. She never got that chance after Catie went missing. *A promise made but never fulfilled.*

"You're doing your best, Jose. This is a tricky case. Mitch Fowler may be concealing what he knows. Or, maybe he knows nothing. The truth will come out one way or another," Sister Maggie replied.

Sister Maggie and Jose discussed the case against the three AHN members. "At least all three men will be put away for a decent number of years," Jose added.

When they finished their lunch, Sister Maggie and Jose walked out to the parking lot together. "Where are you going from here?" Jose asked.

"I have to return to the convent. I have a PowerPoint presentation to prepare for a community meeting next week," Sister Maggie said.

"I didn't realize you drove into Indianapolis from New Hope just to have lunch with me," Jose lamented.

"A forty-five-minute drive is not very long. It's also my turn to buy groceries. On the way back, I'll shop," said Sister Maggie. "I'll be back in Indy tomorrow because I have an appointment with our cat's vet, Dale Wells. His wife suffered a miscarriage the other day," Sister Maggie said. "I'll stop by to see her as well."

"I'm sure your visit will lift her spirits," he said.

"She's a strong young woman. She needs someone to talk to."

Jose handed Sister Maggie an envelope.

"What's this?" Sister Maggie asked. She opened it and her eyes widened at the five-thousand-dollar check.

"Marisol and I want you to use this money for your work with the poor."

"Jose, this is a very generous donation. Thank you so much. I can assure you the Adorers of Divine Love will direct the funds to our poorest mission," she said.

Jose walked Sister Maggie to her vehicle. "It's a shame the Kings and Fowler are out on bail," Jose said as he straightened his blue-and-white striped tie. "Fowler is probably getting a drug fix as we speak," he said. "I need to locate the lowlife's whereabouts."

Sister Maggie realized Jose was already trying to figure out a way to haul Fowler back into jail.

"I bet Frank King and his son are furious at Fowler. He'd probably be safer in jail and protected from those two."

"Maybe I can help him along," Jose said with a grin. "For his own safety, of course."

Sister Maggie chuckled. "Thank you for lunch and for your generous donation. Please give my thanks and love to Marisol. I hope we can have a nice visit soon."

"I will." Jose knocked on the hood of the car. "Take care, Sister Maggie. I'll keep you in the loop."

Sister Maggie watched as Jose walked toward his car. She sat in her car with the driver's door open as she checked her voicemails.

"Sister Maggie, this is Mel Mendez from Florida. I have some information that might interest you on the topic we discussed. Please feel free to call me at your convenience."

She jumped when the car door swung wide. Looking up, she saw Dylan King with his hands on the door frame. *Steady on Clancy.* She knew what Dylan King looked like from news photos, but he had no idea who she was.

"Can I help you?" Sister Maggie asked in a polite but firm voice.

"I saw you coming out of the restaurant wearing the same funny outfit that that nosy chick had on when she and her boyfriend started sniffing around my dad's warehouse. I bet you probably know her, don't you? I heard they were in a bad car accident. I wanted to know how they were doing," Dylan said with a smirk.

Sister Maggie's eyes narrowed. She was spitting mad. "Do you mean the car accident you purposely caused when you forced one of our sisters and her cousin off the road?"

He shrugged. "I never went near them."

"You can rest assured they are hale and hearty and ready to testify against you and *your* friend, Mr. Fowler."

King shook his head. "Why would they do such a stupid thing?"

"Because actions have consequences," Sister Maggie stated. From the corner of her eye, she saw Jose exit his car and stride toward them. "By the way, see that man walking toward us? He's a cop. Now get your hands off my car."

King lifted both hands in front of him and stepped back. He glanced at Jose and then turned back to Sister Maggie. "You have a nice day, ma'am. Drive safe." He turned and strode away.

CHAPTER TWENTY-THREE

May 8, 5:35 p.m.
Vespers at Our Lady of Guadalupe Convent
New Hope, Indiana

"God, come to my assistance," chanted Sister Mary Frances.

"Lord, make haste to help me," Sisters Ruthie, Rose Marie, and Mary Felicia in unison.

Sister Maggie entered the chapel a few minutes late for Evening Prayer. She quickly genuflected and slipped silently into her pew next to Sister Mary Felicia. Sister Mary Felicia intoned the opening hymn, "Amazing Grace."

Sister Mary Frances chanted the first antiphon that preceded Psalm 62. The four sisters alternated their chanting of the stanzas from Psalm 62 as well as the other two Psalms.

When they finished Evening Prayer, the sisters had twenty minutes of silent prayerful meditation.

Sister Maggie had trouble meditating. She was distracted by all kinds of thoughts, starting with Jose Torres's report that Mitch Fowler had refused to cooperate with the DA and reveal the identity of the person who pulled the trigger of the antique Remington revolver that killed Sam Browning. She tried to expel the memory of Dylan King's attempt to intimidate her while she sat in her car. The nerve of him, warning her that Sister Mary Felicia and Jaime better not testify against him at the trial.

And she was worried about Charlie and Dale. Charlie was grieving the loss of her baby while coping with Dale's confession. And tomorrow, she would take Courtney back to Dale for a follow-up. She had no idea how that might turn out. And she hadn't had a chance to call Mel back.

After dealing with the traffic on her drive back from Indianapolis, grocery shopping, and putting away the perishables before arriving late for prayers, life was still full of important questions and problems that needed attention. Yet, each day was full of the tasks of daily life that needed tending. She wondered how the great philosophers and thinkers had the time to come up with their deep and complex thoughts. *They must have had dirty dishes piling up for days.* She shook her head at her wayward thoughts. The past few weeks had been full of stress. Then again, when was her life not stressful? There was always something or someone to worry about.

She let out a deep sigh, then caught herself. Sister Mary Felicia elbowed her. "Are you okay?" she whispered.

Sister Maggie nodded, but she wasn't okay. She couldn't recollect herself and use the prescribed time in the chapel to pray. She remembered the wise advice of St. Therese of Lisieux on what to do during distractions at prayer. The young saint had written that as soon as she was aware of the distractions, she'd pray for those people who occupied her thoughts. By doing this, they would benefit.

She closed her eyes and prayed for all the people she was worried about. After twenty minutes, Sister Maggie tapped a piece of wood in the pew to signal the end of silent prayers.

Sister Rose Marie concluded, "Let us go in peace."

The sisters left the chapel and went into the convent dining room. There, sitting in Sister Maggie's chair, was Courtney, her favorite neon-yellow toy duck in her mouth. "It's not playtime now, Courtney.

It's dinner time," she said as she picked up the kitten and handed her to Sister Mary Felicia.

"Come, sweet kitty," said Sister Mary Felicia. "I'll get your dinner."

The sisters moved about the kitchen as though in a choreographed dance. Sister Rose Marie brought the meatloaf and mashed potatoes to the table, while Sister Mary Frances brought the salad bowl and green beans, and Sister Ruthie put the finishing touches on her fruit salad for dessert. With the table set, the sisters stood by their chairs and bowed their heads as Sister Maggie said grace. Dinner was usually a casual and informal time for the sisters to talk about their day and share any updates from their work in the community unless they were listening to a spiritual recording or eating in prayerful silence.

"I spoke with Sister Mary Grace the other day," Sister Maggie said. "She mentioned they are opening a new mission in Rwanda. The bishop there has begged her to send at least four sisters to start a school for girls."

"Isn't that the country that had a major genocide in the early nineties?" Sister Rose Marie asked.

"Sure is," replied Sister Mary Frances. "In 1994, nearly a million Tutsis were massacred by the Hutus."

"What caused the genocide?" Sister Mary Felicia asked.

"God's loving presence was expelled from the hearts of many, and the worst of human nature took over. When people forget who they are in God's eyes, atrocities of all kinds become possible," Sister Maggie replied.

"Well said," Sister Ruthie said. "I'd go to Rwanda as a missionary if I were younger."

"Well, you did a lot of good work in your many years in service to God," Sister Mary Frances said. "Now, if you didn't have that CPAP machine we might have suggested that you go."

The sisters glanced at each other, eyes wide.

"I think you might be right, Sister Mary Frances," Sister Ruthie quipped. "I always prided myself on my inner strength, even if it comes in the form of a snore—"

The sudden report of a gunshot cut off Sister Ruthie's words.

"Put your hands up. This is a stickup."

Sister Ruthie gasped and got up from her chair. "What in the world? Are we being robbed? Quick where's my baseball bat?"

The other nuns burst out laughing.

"It's all right, Sister Ruthie," Sister Mary Felicia said. "Courtney is playing with the TV remote again."

Sister Ruthie joined in the laughter, and the nuns finished their evening meal in good humor.

CHAPTER TWENTY-FOUR

May 8, 7:00 p.m.
Our Lady of Guadalupe Convent
New Hope, Indiana

"THANKS FOR GIVING me a hand with the rest of the groceries," Sister Maggie said as Sister Mary Felicia put away the dishwasher detergent.

Sister Maggie groaned as she stretched her shoulders. It had been another stressful day.

"You look like you need to take a load off," the young sister said.

"Well, since you've put it so delicately, I think I will follow your advice shortly." Sister Maggie did something she rarely did—she plugged in the electric kettle to make herself a cup of chamomile tea before going into the convent office to call Mel Mendez.

"Sorry I missed your call, Mel. I'm anxious to hear what you learned," Sister Maggie said as she sipped her hot tea and sat back in her desk chair.

"Sister, I did quite a bit of digging. I actually spoke to the former executive secretary of the founder and head of the company who founded ARS Industrial Supplies. The company letters, ARS, stand for Alexander Raymond Stanley, the name of the founder, but everyone called him Ray. Alice Crenshaw told me she remembered several men who made up the sales team during the expansion of ARS supplies into the first schools and office buildings in Florida some forty-five to fifty years ago. Unfortunately, she couldn't remember their names," Mel said.

Sister Maggie could hear Mel flipping through the pages of her notes. "So I did more research. Originally, there were eight men, but five of them were in their forties or older when they worked for the company, and are now deceased. We can look into them later as well if you like, but in the meantime, we can start with the three former salesmen who were under twenty-five years of age at the time Catie vanished—Calvin and Cody Pierce, and Jim Wade."

Sister Maggie's instincts and her visions told her it could not have been an older man who'd kidnapped Catie. Her money was on Calvin, Cody, or Jim.

"My cousin, Alejandro Reyes, is a private detective and former police officer for the Miami-Dade Police Department," Mel added. "I hope you don't mind, but I called him and asked if he could help."

"That is so kind of you," Sister Maggie said.

"I'm happy to help in any way. Al is pretty unique. He can detect deception more accurately than the most sophisticated lie detector tests. I should mention he and his wife have four boys under the age of sixteen, who at various times have foolishly attempted to tell lies or half-truths. His kids' nickname for him is Deputy Al Dawg."

"Sounds like a great family.

"They are the best."

"I have a sense that one day soon, we'll have closure to Catie's death," Sister Maggie said as she choked back tears.

"I gave Al your cell number. Knowing my cousin, he should have some information for you soon. You can stay with me when you fly down. We built a cute apartment above our garage. Plenty of room for two people if you'd like to bring another sister with you."

"I will definitely do that," Sister Maggie said. "And thanks again for all your help."

Sister Maggie hung up and closed her eyes. What an exhausting day. The drive was all right, but her run-in with Dylan King had thrown her for a loop. Good thing Jose Torres had still been in the parking lot when the altercation happened.

Sister Maggie stared straight ahead at her computer monitor and felt something like an electrical current running through her body. Suddenly, the monitor disappeared. In its place, an image appeared of Catie at the Florida amusement park talking to a young man wearing a sweatshirt with the word "COACH" on the back. He wore a baseball cap turned backward. The images before her reminded her of watching an old silent black-and-white movie.

All of Sister Maggie's attention was on the man talking to Catie. She could see he was tall and thin. Most of his dark hair was hidden under his baseball cap. She watched her twin as she smiled at the young man and showed off the teddy bear she'd won at the coin toss game. They appeared to be chatting about something for a few moments then all of a sudden Sister Maggie saw the young man grab Catie's arm and whisper something in her ear. Catie shook her head no and tried to pull away but he yanked on her arm. Sister Maggie gasped as she saw the flash of a knife glinting in the sun. Catie's eyes widened with fear and she stood frozen to the spot.

The man tossed the stuffed bear into a trash bin near the women's restroom, removed his baseball cap, and used it to conceal the knife. That's when Sister Maggie noticed his dark hair was curly. He forced Catie to walk briskly with him in the direction of the dense crowd.

Catie glanced back over her shoulder, and it was as though she were looking directly at Sister Maggie from the computer screen. Sister Maggie reached out to touch the screen as the image froze and then faded to black.

Oh, Catie. You looked back hoping Josie and I would emerge from the bathroom and run after you to save you...

A wavy of dizziness came over Sister Maggie and the room began to spin, she closed her eyes to get her bearings. When she opened them again she saw that she was no longer sitting in front of the computer screen in the convent office. She was now standing in a tunnel.

A light flared and illuminated a yellow and black sign that read "... *EY TUNNEL. CLEARANCE 13' 9"*.

Sister Maggie realized the tunnel had a name, but she couldn't make out the complete word. The other letters were covered in mud.

The light flared brighter and Sister Maggie saw Catie again, standing underneath the sign. She gestured for Sister Maggie to follow her. Catie walked farther into the tunnel and then stopped. She leaned against the wall, drawing Sister Maggie's attention to the dirty, chipped rock behind her. Catie pointed to the opposite end of the tunnel. Farther down, the tunnel was made of smooth white tiles, not the dirty rocks where Catie stood.

"Catie, please can you tell me more? Where is this tunnel?"

The blare of a horn sounded, and Sister Maggie turned toward the sound. She blinked as bright lights flashed before her eyes. She realized a truck was barreling toward her as she stood in the middle of the tunnel. A scream tore itself from her throat, and she covered her face with her hands.

Sister Maggie's eyes flew open, and she gasped. A soft and furry paw was touching her face. She covered the little paw with her hand and felt the wetness on her own cheeks. Her eyes looked into the face of the kitten, who stared intently at her. Courtney meowed and nuzzled its head against Sister Maggie's neck.

"You sweet girl," Sister Maggie said as she lifted Courtney and cuddled her. "Thank you for coming to my rescue."

The cat continued to purr against Sister Maggie's neck.

She glanced at her wristwatch and noted a half-hour had passed since her call to Mel.

Sister Maggie closed her eyes once again with Courtney in her lap. She breathed deeply, trying to calm her nerves. After a few moments, she opened the drawer of her bedside table and removed her leather journal. As she had done in the past, she jotted down what she had learned in her visions. She even sketched the white tiles that were shown to her by her sister.

"Are you okay?"

Sister Maggie turned to look at Sister Mary Felicia, who had just walked into the office. Sister Maggie nodded and pointed to the kitten. "I fell asleep at the desk. Courtney decided to join me."

"Why not join us in the community room? Sister Mary Frances is going to show us the video from the Youth Talent Show a few weeks back. And Sister Ruthie warmed up a batch of oatmeal cookies she had in the freezer."

Sister Maggie lifted Courtney and nuzzled her nose against the cat's snout. "How about watching a video, runt?"

Courtney meowed.

"I think the cookies decided it." Sister Maggie chuckled. "I'll be there in a moment."

"Great." Sister Mary Felicia smiled as she turned to walk out of the office.

Sister Maggie set the kitten on the desk, noticing how her black fur glistened in the glow of the desk lamp. Then she recalled a detail from her vision that she'd missed before. When he'd held up the knife, there was a flash of a dark marking on his right arm.

Could it have been a tattoo?

Tattoos were common today, and many people sported them, but she wondered if they were as common almost fifty years ago. When Sister Maggie began her work at St. Malachy, she remembered some of the war veterans had tattoos on their forearms. Father O'Connor had also taught a Bible study class for ex-cons—men who'd spent time in prison. Sister Maggie recalled most of them sported tattoos as well. *Could the man who took Catie have been in the military? Could he have spent time in prison?*

Whoever you are, I'll find you...

CHAPTER TWENTY-FIVE

May 12, 2:00 p.m.
Home of Dale and Charlie Wells
Indianapolis, Indiana

"How is Charlie today?" asked Sister Maggie as she entered the front hallway of the Wells's ranch house.

"Much better," Dale said. "She's just taking a nap. We had quite the morning. I know Charlie told you we began the paperwork last year with an adoption agency when Charlie was unable to conceive. And just this morning we got a phone call about a baby boy in Colombia. His parents died a couple of months ago in a mudslide caused by torrential rains. In fact, his entire village was destroyed. Miraculously, a teenage girl rescued the baby. He was in a basket up in a tree. His father must have put him there to keep him safe."

"Oh, to have such a tragedy turn into such a joyful end," Sister Maggie said, holding her hands up in prayer. Those poor people had so little, and in a matter of hours, lost everything—life can be so fragile. But how wonderful that the baby will have a fresh start here with you and Charlie."

"In a way, it feels like a miracle—and a gift," Dale said, his voice heavy with emotion.

And you're right, Sister Maggie, sometimes we forget how precious life is." He led Sister Maggie into the living room. "I made some coffee if you'd like some."

"Maybe later," Maggie said. "I've already had my coffee quota for the day." Although she wanted to know more about the infant boy and the pending adoption, her visit had another purpose. She needed to get to the truth. "Why don't the two of us chat." She strolled to the gun cabinets. "You inherited a formidable gun collection from your father." Once again, she scanned the guns on display. Each designated spot had a gun.

"Many of the antique guns still function," Dale said as he unlocked one of the cabinets. He took out what looked like an old cowboy gun. "For example, this gun was probably used by a cowboy in the Wild West. I've never fired it, but it's in such great condition it probably would hit its target successfully. No bullets in the chamber, of course."

"You must have had many interesting conversations with your father about guns," remarked Sister Maggie as she carefully watched Dale's face.

"Actually, my father and I rarely spoke," Dale said as he returned the gun to the cabinet.

"Your mother still lives in Brooklyn and attends St. Malachy's," she said in Spanish.

Dale smiled. "*Es verdad*," he said, meaning "it's true." He continued in English. "She spent many years catering to her husband."

Sister Maggie couldn't help but hear the sarcasm in Dale's voice. "I wonder why you used the word 'catering' to describe how your mother related to your father. Marriage is supposed to be a partnership between a man and a woman, not a master and servant relationship."

Dale pursed his lips and then said, "My mother is a saint. I admit it —when it came to my father, she was more like a martyr. He didn't deserve her."

"I see," Sister Maggie said. "Do you mind if we sit for a bit? When you get to my age, you think you can still do everything you used to do, but your body thinks otherwise."

"Of course," Dale replied as he led the way to the seating area. Dale offered her a seat in one of the armchairs. He sat opposite her.

Sister Maggie adjusted her white scapular and folded her hands in her lap. "The other day I was here, Charlie was beside herself with grief about the miscarriage. She even blamed herself for it. She said God was punishing her for her sin." Sister Maggie stared into Dale's dark green eyes.

"God wasn't punishing her. He was punishing me!" Dale blurted out.

Sister Maggie leaned forward. "No. You're wrong, Dale. God extended his loving embrace to your baby. He wasn't punishing either of you. It's a fact of life we're all going to die. Whether we are babies in the womb, infants already born, or if we make it to 100—death is something we all must face. But the years we spend on this earth are like a snap of the fingers in the light of eternity," Sister Maggie stressed.

Dale's eyes skittered away from her. He ran his hands through his hair and sighed.

"I'm not God's spokeswoman, but I know God loves us unconditionally. And when we pass on, we return back to His light," Sister Maggie said. "And if we don't allow the light in, then the darkness will win out."

Dale shook his head. "I don't have your depth of faith," he said. "You sound like my mother whenever she spoke to me about God's will."

"Your mother was right. What I am telling you is the same as what your mother told you. Charlie said you have a secret that is killing you—"

"She told you?" Dale met Sister Maggie's gaze. "She—she had no right to tell you something I told her in confidence."

"She has every right to share what she believes will kill you," Sister Maggie said grimly. "You were contemplating suicide. Charlie was beside herself with grief and sorrow. First losing your baby, and then the thought of losing you to suicide overwhelmed her."

Dale clenched his hands in his lap. "My father was a cruel and heartless man. He used my mother and made a fool out of her. He was a womanizer and had no regrets until he faced death. He begged her forgiveness. Being a woman of faith, she forgave him on his death bed. The coward was afraid to die and go to Hell for his sins."

"He may have been a coward and afraid of eternal punishment, but it forced him to confront his sins against your mother. He begged her forgiveness and, I assume, God's forgiveness. He knew that when we cross from time to eternity, there is something called divine justice, but he wanted mercy," Sister Maggie said.

A sob escaped Dale, and he covered his mouth.

"Your mother showed you the meaning of unconditional love and mercy," she said in a gentle voice. Out of the corner of her eye, Sister Maggie saw Charlie standing at the doorway of the living room. She had no idea how much Charlie had heard, but in the next moment, Charlie rushed forward and sat on the arm of Dale's chair. She wrapped her arms around him and began to cry.

"Dale, this is all my fault. If I hadn't had that affair with Sam after our breakup—"

"No. None of this is your fault." Dale interrupted her, pulling her tightly against him. "I was a fool. I was jealous of Sam, and I snapped. I thought of you in his arms, and it sent me over the edge."

Sister Maggie watched as Charlie placed her husband's face in her hands. "My love, the thought of losing you—I couldn't bear it. I'm equally to blame for Sam's death," Charlie said.

"Did you kill Sam?" Sister Maggie asked Dale.

CHAPTER TWENTY-SIX

May 12, 2:30 p.m.
Home of Dale and Charlie Wells
Indianapolis, Indiana

Dale leaned back but kept his arms around Charlie. "I'd just come from buying an antique Remington revolver from a gun shop in town. It was in beautiful condition with a mother-of-pearl handle. I knew Charlie was at the fundraiser that night, so I planned to surprise her and pick her up when it was over."

"Go on," Sister Maggie said in a soft voice.

"I wasn't happy that Charlie and Sam were working together again. I thought he'd maneuvered his transfer to Indianapolis so he could be near her. I—I imagined the worst of intentions. I decided to pay him a visit before picking Charlie up." Dale shifted in the chair and, turning his head, stared into his wife's light green eyes. "Sweetheart, I did forgive you, but I thought Sam was out to destroy our marriage. I just wanted to talk to him."

"What did you do when you arrived at the zoo?" Sister Maggie asked.

Dale kept looking into his wife's eyes. "He was outside the orangutan exhibit, so I called out to him. He was as friendly as could be. He asked if I was going to the fundraising event. When I told him I was at the zoo to settle a score with him, he just stared at me. I asked him why he came to the Indiana State Zoo. He laughed and said he wanted to be close to Leo and work with him on communication skills. That's when I lost it," said Dale.

Dale grasped Charlie's hand in his. "I told Sam I thought he was there to reclaim Charlie. Sam denied it and said he'd made a mistake in judgment and he was no threat to our marriage. But I didn't believe him," Dale said.

"Sam told you the truth," Charlie said, her voice thick with emotion.

"I know that now that I can think clearly. But a few weeks ago, I was full of anger and jealousy. "

Charlie laid her hand on Dale's face. "Go on, Dale. Tell Sister Maggie what happened."

Dale took out a photo from his pocket and handed it to Sister Maggie.

The picture showed Charlie signing to Leo while Sam stood beside them, a big smile on his face.

"That photo convinced me Sam was in love with Charlie. He asked me to walk with him back to his office. He wanted to pick up one of Leo's favorite toys. I think he wanted to go to his office to calm me down. When I got to his office, there it was, that same photo framed and sitting on Sam's desk. I completely lost it. Even while Sam was explaining to me that his relationship with Charlie was purely professional and that his commitment to Leo had made him move back to a city he'd sworn never to return to—I didn't believe him. All I could see was his big smile in that photo. Everything he said to me sounded like a lie. Like he was making a fool out of me. As we walked back out to the enclosure, he kept trying to reassure me he didn't want any more than a working relationship with my wife. But I was lost in a rage. The more he talked, the angrier I became."

"What happened next?" Sister Maggie asked.

"I took out my gun and ordered Sam to get on his knees." Dale shook his head as if to erase the memory from his mind. "Sam knelt down on the ground and looked up at me. He—he said he wished only the best for Charlie, that he regretted the one-night stand. I waved the gun around. I—I just wanted to scare him. I'd only just bought the gun. I—I didn't think to check it for bullets. I know it was stupid. But I wasn't thinking straight that day."

Charlie was sobbing now, her head on Dale's shoulder.

Dale's lips trembled as he held Charlie close to his side.

"Dale, please tell me. Unburden yourself," Sister Maggie said.

"I was saying crazy things—accusing him of being selfish and a coward for trying to break up a marriage. I was in this sort of red haze of anger…Then Sam did something that threw me for a loop. He—he grabbed hold of the gun and pressed the muzzle against his forehead. He said, 'Go ahead and shoot me. I deserve it.' Even in my anger, I was still shocked at what he was saying…He pulled at my wrist as he started to get up— and the gun it—it went off."

Dale was staring straight ahead as though he were watching the horrible moment once more. Sister Maggie clenched the arms of the chair, feeling as though she, too, were there, watching events unfold.

"The bullet penetrated his head between his eyes. He fell to my feet. It was so surreal. I stood frozen in place until I realized I needed to check for signs of life. But it was no use. He was already dead. No pulse, no heartbeat. Nothing.

"No one was around, so I took off. I knew Frank King bought and sold antique guns out of his warehouse—it was illegal—but a lot of gun owners don't care, especially if they're die-hard collectors. I only ever bought guns legally, but I didn't know what to do. I knew if I sold the gun to them, it would probably have been resold in a matter of days. I just wanted to get rid of it. I never wanted to lay eyes on it again," said Dale.

"Who bought the gun from you at the warehouse?" Sister Maggie asked. "Was it Frank King?"

"Frank wasn't even there. His son Dylan was there with Mitch Fowler. They were just sitting around drinking beer in the office. Mitch bought it from me for a fraction of what I'd paid at the gun store. Frank's son, Dylan was there for the exchange. Mitch checked the chamber for bullets and noted it was empty. But, when he put the gun to his nose, he said it smelled like it had been fired recently. I lied and told him I had no idea who the previous owner was or who might have used it," Dale said.

"Tell me again why you sold the gun," Sister Maggie said.

"Because the sight of it made me sick. I couldn't stand to look at the gun and think of Sam with a bullet in his head," said Dale.

Sister Maggie leaned forward. "Dale, you have to turn yourself in. The circumstances surrounding the shooting make a world of difference. You had no intent to murder Sam. You didn't know the gun was loaded, and your jealousy clouded your judgment. You need to find a good lawyer who can help you do the right thing," Sister Maggie urged.

"What about my work and the clinic? What about this little boy we want to adopt?" Dale's gaze was full of misery.

"Dale, it's likely you could be charged with negligent homicide. I'm no lawyer, but what I do know is that in all criminally negligent homicides, the prosecution has to prove the person was aware of the risk associated with his or her actions. In your case, pulling the trigger was not an intentional act to kill Sam. You thought the storekeeper sold you an unloaded gun. Yes, you were foolish not to have checked the gun after you bought it. But you weren't in your right mind. You weren't exactly thinking clearly," Sister Maggie concluded.

"Honey, I'll be at your side through all this. You won't be alone—ever," Charlie said.

Sister Maggie held the photo up. "This photo. You mentioned you saw it on Sam's desk in a frame. Did you go back to retrieve it? How did you come by it here?"

"Charlie was arranging pictures for a photo album, and I saw it in a pile of work photos. She said it was a picture from when she worked at the New York Zoo. She'd forgotten she had it. I simply took it."

"And when you saw that same photo in a frame on Sam's desk, in such a prominent place—"

"I lost it completely," Dale said interrupting Sister Maggie.

"I'm so sorry," Charlie said in a broken whisper. "If it hadn't been for that photo..."

"It's all right, honey," Dale said. "None of this is your fault."

"Dale, when your father was on his death bed and asked you for forgiveness, what words did he use?" Sister Maggie asked.

"He said he regretted all those one-night stands."

"And you walked out of the hospital without forgiving him?"

"Yes."

"Dale, what would your sainted mother tell you to do in this situation?" asked Sister Maggie.

Dale looked at Sister Maggie. His eyes widened as though he were seeing the truth for the first time. "She'd tell me to do the right thing for the right reason. I'll go to the police."

"My own dear mother, Mama Lulu, taught me and my siblings that doing the right thing may come at a cost, but it's never optional."

CHAPTER TWENTY-SEVEN

May 20, 11:45 a.m.
Indianapolis International Airport
Indianapolis, Indiana

"HURRY, Sister Maggie. Our flight is boarding," shouted Sister Mary Felicia, waving from the end of the line at the boarding terminal.

Sister Maggie jogged up to Sister Mary Felicia, trying to catch her breath.

"I thought you were right behind me," Sister Mary Felicia said. "What happened?"

"The security officer at the X-ray machine made me open my luggage. He said he saw something that looked suspicious," Sister Maggie grumbled. "It turned out to be one of Courtney's toys. The officer said it looked like a dead animal. Really? Now, what would a nun be doing with a carcass in her suitcase?"

Sister Mary Felicia chuckled. "Which toy?"

"That neon-yellow duck." Sister Maggie rolled her eyes. "The runt was playing by my suitcase last night. She probably slipped the duck in when I wasn't looking. I got a phone call from Dale and Charlie this morning and was running late, and I just ended up throwing my things into the suitcase. I never noticed the darn toy."

The sisters made their way onto the boarding platform and found their seats in the middle of the plane.

"This is an awfully small jet," Sister Maggie said. She unzipped her carry-on and pulled out a shawl, then stowed the suitcase in the compartment above their seats. She was always cold on flights and never traveled without her shawl.

"The price was right," said Sister Mary Felicia, settling into the window seat. Sister Maggie always preferred the aisle in case she had to go to the restroom.

"Are you sure it's safe? It reminds me more of a bus with wings than a jet."

"Don't worry, I got us travel insurance." Sister Mary Felicia winked. "Just in case."

"Well, doesn't that make me feel a whole lot better." Sister Maggie fumbled with her seatbelt. Voluminous habits and airplane seatbelts did not go well together. And she was no longer as slim as she used to be. *I've got to lay off those baked goods when I do home visits.*

"What was the phone call about?" Sister Mary Felicia asked.

"Dale and Charlie called me," Sister Maggie replied, heaving a deep sigh. "Dale said he spoke with David Moore, the criminal defense lawyer I recommended. Given that Dale is an upstanding citizen with no prior record who contributes to the community and has a thriving veterinary clinic with plenty of people who can vouch for him, David will most likely get Dale a reduced sentence or perhaps even probation involving community service and anger management therapy."

"That's good news, indeed," Sister Mary Felicia said.

"But, their pending adoption is now up in the air given the circumstances."

"I hope everything works out for them," Sister Mary Felicia said. "They're good people. It was a terrible and tragic mistake."

"It certainly was. But Dale and Charlie are determined to get through this together."

"I just can't fathom Sam doing something like that with the gun and asking Dale to pull the trigger."

"From what Charlie told me about Sam's past, he was indeed a troubled soul," Sister Maggie said. "He confided in Charlie about a friend of his in college, a remarkable young man and star athlete who basically saved his life and helped him escape the Alliance of Heritage Nationalists. This young man was killed in a car crash on a rainy night while driving home from work. Sam believed that Dylan King and Mitch Fowler along with another crony, ran that young man off the road. He was Nigerian-born, and had immigrated to the United States because of tribal violence."

Sister Mary Felicia gasped. "You mean the AHN has a history of doing this?"

Sister Maggie nodded. "Before you and I left for Miami, I told Charlie and Dale to speak to Jose Torres about this. At the time, the police ruled it as an accident, but now they can go back and interview people who knew them in college—and perhaps find something they'd missed the first time because they hadn't been looking at it as a homicide investigation."

"And it can certainly establish a history of violence with King and Fowler."

"God knows how many other victims are out there from their cruel and reckless actions."

"Well, Jaime and I will do our part." Sister Mary Felicia nodded. "We are all set to testify."

Sister Maggie smiled. "And how are you doing? With everything going on the past few weeks, we haven't had a good catch-up."

Sister Mary Felicia turned slightly in her seat to face Sister Maggie. "Physically, I'm back to normal. Emotionally, I still have flashbacks of the crash that killed my brother and chauffeur. I'll talk to my Uncle Bob about it. He helped me deal with that awful period of my life following the crash. He'll be in Indianapolis next week to visit some seminarians, and we'll have time to talk."

"That's good to hear. I'm sure talking to your uncle will help."

A friendly voice said above them, "Would you care for a drink to go with your pretzels?" The stewardess had reached their seat with the refreshment trolley and handed them each a napkin and the packaged snacks.

"I'll have a diet cola," Sister Mary Felicia said.

"Club soda for me," Sister Maggie added.

"There you go," the stewardess smiled, handing them each a plastic glass.

"Thank you, dear," Sister Maggie said.

"Oh, Sister, I believe you dropped this." The stewardess placed a neon-yellow duck onto the seat-back tray and gave it a little squeeze. "By the way, I have two cats, and you wouldn't believe the things I find in my travel bag."

CHAPTER TWENTY-EIGHT

May 20, 3:40 p.m.
Miami International Airport

"SISTER MAGGIE, OVER HERE." A young woman with shoulder-length black hair waved at them. Mel Gonzalez-Mendez, the former youth group member from St. Malachy Parish, was as stunning as ever. Sister Maggie remembered all the teenage boys used to flock around Mel, in those youth group days. And things certainly hadn't changed. Heads turned as Mel approached them.

Sister Maggie and Mel embraced.

"This is Sister Mary Felicia, our associate vocations director." Sister Maggie beamed proudly as she presented the young sister to Mel.

Mel's mouth opened wide. "You're *the* Casey Bauer. I was one of your die-hard fans for years. You're more beautiful now in your blue and white habit and veil than when you were as a pop star. I can't wait to introduce you to my three daughters," said Mel.

"You have three girls?" asked Sister Mary Felicia.

"Twelve, fourteen, and seventeen. They are my direct ticket to Heaven." Mel rolled her eyes. "I see you both brought your luggage on board." Mel reached for Sister Maggie's overnight bag, but Sister Maggie shook her head.

"It's not heavy, Mel. Actually, it's much lighter now that the neon yellow duck is sitting in Sister Mary Felicia's bag," she joked.

"A duck?" asked Mel.

"I'll tell you all about it later."

As the women left the airport terminal, Mel told them her cousin Al was waiting for them outside by his blue van.

Mel waved to her cousin. "Al just got back in his van and is headed this way," she said.

After formal introductions were made, Sister Maggie was invited to sit in the passenger seat next to Al.

"Thank you for your willingness to help me with my investigation. For your pro bono work, you can count on the prayers of the Adorers of Divine Love," said Sister Maggie.

"I appreciate the prayers. I especially need them for my autistic son, Jerry. My wife and I have four high-energy boys, but Jerry is a special needs kid and sometimes it can be more demanding," Al said.

"You shall have our prayers for your family and especially your son Jerry," Sister Mary Felicia said.

"Mel told me you tracked down the whereabouts of three men employed by ARS Industrial Cleaning Supplies at the time Catie was kidnapped," said Sister Maggie.

"Correct. Jim Wade is the only one of the three who still lives in the Miami area. He's not the killer, but he is definitely someone you need to meet," emphasized Al.

Sister Maggie leaned toward Al. "Are you sure he's not the killer?

"I am."

"And where do the Pierce brothers live?"

"Calvin lived in Atlanta, Georgia, and Cody is in Brooklyn, New York."

"This makes things more complicated." Sister Maggie sighed as she tried to process the information Al shared.

Tilting his head in Sister Maggie's direction, Al added, "It's even more complicated, I'm afraid. Calvin died two days ago from a drug overdose—"

"Oh no!" Sister Maggie interjected.

"I know you're disappointed, but we need to be patient," Al continued. "I think it's important for you to speak with Jim Wade first, regardless of who your sister's killer is."

Sister Maggie was confused by Al's comment but she was more frustrated than anything else. She had constructed in her mind a scenario in which she would learn who killed Catie and be present as the police arrested him. And it would all happen over the next few days. So many years had gone by…Her father passed away ten years ago, never having known who his daughter's killer was. Sister Maggie couldn't bear it if Mama Lulu joined him before they had closure. She needed to find the killer so her entire family could finally lay Catie to rest.

Sister Mary Felicia leaned forward from the back seat and gently touched her arm. "Everything will be okay."

Sister Maggie nodded.

"Together, we'll put the pieces of the puzzle together," Al said. "Step one is to talk to Jim Wade. You have to trust me."

"I do trust you. But we're talking about fifty years ago. The local police force couldn't find the killer. My dad was a police captain, and he couldn't track down the killer. My brothers are cops, and they couldn't either. All we have to go on are my gut feelings and your investigative skills on a cold case that is only now beginning to thaw."

"We'll keep helping you, Sister Maggie," Mel said in a reassuring voice. You and your family deserve justice."

"Thank you, both," Sister Maggie said. "I apologize for my outburst."

"I would feel the same way in your situation," Al said.

"Can you tell me anything more about Calvin Pierce?"

"He did twelve years in Wallington Federal Prison in Atlanta for drug trafficking and was released just last week," Al said.

"He certainly wasted no time getting back into drugs," Mel added.

"He was charged with human trafficking twelve years ago along with the drug trafficking offense," Al continued. "But there wasn't enough evidence to convict him on both counts."

"Human trafficking?" Sister Maggie said. "He could have been involved in any number of things—selling women and children as sex slaves, organ-harvesting for transplants..."

"What kind of horrible people can do such things?" Sister Mary Felicia said.

"Human traffickers are the slime of the earth," Al agreed. "At any given moment, some thirty million victims are abducted worldwide."

Sister Maggie sighed. "What about Cody Pierce?"

"Cody is in a Catholic nursing home in Brooklyn," Al replied. "He was penniless and an invalid by the time he was accepted by the Sisters of the Elderly Sick. He'd been in and out of jail through the decades. Let's hope he got some religion with the good sisters. His crime of preference was to rough up people who failed to pay their illegal gambling debts to a certain notorious Mafia don in Brooklyn."

Sister Maggie shook her head at the irony of it. "All this time he was right under my nose in Brooklyn. My whole family lives in New York. To think we might have tracked him down if only we'd known."

"What about Jim Wade?" Sister Mary Felicia asked.

"He's a minister just outside of Miami," Al said.

Sister Maggie's head was spinning. Her hope that this trip would lead her to the truth was disintegrating before her eyes. Thank goodness she hadn't told her brothers or Mama Lulu about it. She wanted to spare everyone the pain and anguish of yet another dead end.

"When are we going to see the Reverend Wade?" asked Sister Maggie.

"Tomorrow morning," Al said.

Seconds passed as Al maneuvered around a pair of vehicles driving far slower than the speed limit. Sure enough, a gray-haired driver occupied each driver's seat, one so short her head was barely level with the steering wheel. *At least I'll never have to worry about shrinking down to that height,* thought Sister Maggie.

"Sister Maggie, I remember something you taught me when I was in the parish youth group," Mel said. "You taught me that everything happens for a reason in life. Sometimes what happens prepares us for things to come. Other times, what happens changes our way of thinking or our perception of reality. You said when things happen for a reason, God is preparing us to be more empathetic, sympathetic, and open to spiritual growth. The identity of Catie's killer may not come tomorrow, but both Al and I truly believe this unusual unfolding of events is happening for a reason. The truth will come to light at the right time, which is always God's time."

Sister Maggie closed her eyes to hold back the tears. What Mel said was true.

"Are you all right, Sister Maggie?" Sister Mary Felicia asked.

Sister Maggie took a deep breath and turned to the three concerned faces watching her. "To paraphrase the scriptures, a disciple is not greater than his or her teacher, but everyone, when fully trained, will be like his or her teacher. Thank you, Mel, you've reminded me that even after all these years, I still have a lot to learn."

"Sister Maggie, you're the wisest woman I know," Sister Mary Felicia said.

"Thank you. I'll try to stay as objective as I can. In the meantime, this wise woman's stomach is grumbling. I'm looking forward to that delicious homemade Puerto Rican dinner you mentioned, Mel."

CHAPTER TWENTY-NINE

May 20, 7:00 p.m.
Home of Melissa Gonzalez-Mendez
Miami, Florida

"Who wants seconds?"

"I do." Sister Maggie and Sister Mary Felicia both said at the same time. Jessica, Paula, and Brenda, Mel's three daughters, smiled with pride since they had prepared the dinner.

"Mom knew you loved Puerto Rican food," said Brenda, the youngest of the three girls.

"Oh, I do indeed," Sister Maggie said. "I remember your grandmother used to prepare special dishes for the sisters from time to time —*arroz con gandules, mofongo,* and *pasteles*. How is she doing?"

"Oh, Grandma Gloria and my uncle Al's parents went on a Caribbean Cruise. They're having a blast," replied Brenda.

"Good to hear it. I'm glad she's enjoying her retirement," Sister Maggie said.

"I hope your meeting with Jim Wade goes well tomorrow," Mel's husband Gustavo said. "Some of my construction workers have known Jim for years. They have the greatest respect for him."

"I hope he can help enlighten us," Sister Maggie said, taking a forkful of *pernil* and a spoonful of rice. She reminded herself to be patient, but she was on pins and needles. She hoped this minister had some answers for her.

"Your mom invited me to sing some of my old songs after dinner," said Sister Mary Felicia to the girls. "She said all three of you have beautiful voices. Do you want to sing backup?"

The girls jumped in their seats, and their excited squeals answered for them.

After the delicious meal, Gustavo offered to clean up and load the dishwasher. "I may be a Latino man, but I'm outnumbered in this house," he joked.

"You're the best husband and dad there is," Mel said, giving him a kiss on the cheek.

"Mommy, you're kissing Daddy in front of two nuns," Jessica, the eldest, said with a gasp.

"Showing affection in front of our children is a positive thing, is it not, Sister Maggie?" Mel winked.

"It certainly is," Sister Maggie replied with a wink back. "Your parents love each other very much. They're setting an example."

"Okay, but maybe they could ease up on setting an example when our friends are over," Paula said with an eye roll.

Arm in arm, Mel and the three girls escorted Sister Mary Felicia and Sister Maggie to the family room.

Sister Mary Felicia began the entertainment for the evening by singing the number one hits for which she was famous more than a decade earlier. She invited the girls to sing the words she had printed out for them.

"These are great songs," Jessica said.

"The enthusiasm from Mel's girls proves your songs live on in the hearts of another generation," Sister Maggie said.

Sister Mary Felicia smiled. "It humbles me to know there still is an audience that appreciates my music." She proceeded to tell her young fans that she was completing a Christian album of contemporary and traditional songs. "I hope you'll enjoy my new music," Sister Mary

Felicia said. "If and when I perform again for charity, I hope the Mendez family will join the Adorers of Divine Love in the front row."

By half-past ten, Sister Maggie was beat. Between the stress of the past few weeks and the flight to Miami, it was all she could do to stay awake. She and Sister Mary Felicia said their goodnights and made their way to the cozy garage apartment.

"Okay, what's up, Sister Maggie?" Sister Mary Felicia asked. "You're usually the belle of the ball, but you seemed subdued this evening. Are you still worried about what we'll find out?"

"The meeting with Jim Wade tomorrow concerns me," Sister Maggie replied. "I'm worried about what I may learn about Red's killer. Was he a pedophile or a human trafficker? Either possibility makes my stomach churn."

"You've been preparing for decades to discover the truth about your sister's abduction. You have to trust that somehow justice will be served, and you and your family will finally have closure."

"I hope so."

"You are going to tell your brothers what you learn from Jim Wade, right?"

"Of course," Sister Maggie said. *At some point...*

CHAPTER THIRTY

May 21, 9:00 a.m.
St. Thomas Aquinas Church
Miami, Florida

Sister Maggie greeted the pastor after morning Mass at the small church just ten minutes from Mel and Gustavo Mendez's house.

"Thank you, Padre Guillermo, for your reflection this morning on fear and faith. It's true. Our hearts can't be filled with fear and faith at the same time," Sister Maggie said.

The young priest smiled at Sister Maggie. "And, fear disappears when love pushes it away."

Sister Maggie nodded at the priest. "You're wise beyond your years," she said as the priest escorted her and Sister Mary Felicia out to the parking area.

"Ready to meet Jim Wade?" Al asked.

"Ready and willing," Sister Maggie replied.

Al drove to a small mission-style blue stucco house with a lovely flower garden in the front. An older woman who appeared to be biracial greeted them at the front door, a cane in her right hand. "You must be Sister Maggie. Please come in. My husband is inside. My name is Elizabeth Wade."

Sister Maggie greeted the elderly woman and introduced Sister Mary Felicia.

"Thank you, Elizabeth, for making this visit possible," Al said. "Sister Maggie is eager to meet Reverend Wade and get another step closer to finding out what happened to her twin all those years ago."

Elizabeth's smile was genuine. "My husband and I have been praying for you from the time Al approached us," she said as she led them down a small hallway.

Jim Wade was sitting in a wheelchair reading the Bible. He looked up and smiled at them. "Good morning, Sisters. Good morning, Al," Jim said. "Excuse me if I don't get up to greet you. I have multiple sclerosis. When I have a flare, I need to use this contraption," he said as he tapped the arm of his wheelchair.

"Please have a seat and make yourselves comfortable," Elizabeth said, gesturing to the sofa. "May I offer you something to drink?"

Al held up his hand. "We all had a big breakfast at Mel's but thank you."

Jim Wade turned to Sister Maggie. "Al told me about your sister Catie and her abduction at the amusement park all those years ago. I may be able to shed some light on what may have happened to her."

Elizabeth walked to the armchair next to Jim and sat beside him.

Jim Wade rolled up the sleeve of his beige lightweight cardigan sweater to reveal a white supremacist symbol. "I was told I could have this Valknot tattoo removed. I chose to keep it. It's known as the *knot of the slain*," he said as he took his wife's hand. "Back when I was young and stupid, I belonged to the AHN, better known as the Alliance of Heritage Nationalists. The organization is nationwide but the group I belonged to was based in Indiana.

Sister Maggie's eyes widened as she beheld the tattoo. One of her recent visions had revealed a tattoo on the arm of Catie's abductor. Now she knew what it was—the Valknot. Even more disconcerting—it was the same tattoo that Sam had had on his arm. She exchanged a glance with Sister Mary Felicia. "We've come to know quite a lot about the AHN from a recent murder that happened back home."

"It's terrible, what they believe. I've spent these past many years spreading the good news of the gospel and trying to help people see the light. Why, if I hadn't met my Lizzy here, I think I would have ended up on the road to ruin. Tell them, Lizzy," said Jim.

Lizzy squeezed her husband's hand. "I was working as a registered nurse at the Florida General Hospital when I met Jim. He was here on vacation. I was on duty at the hospital when the paramedics wheeled Jim in on a stretcher. He'd been in a terrible motorcycle accident. I was his nurse. As you can see, I'm biracial. My mother was white, and my father, African American. Jim's injuries from the motorcycle accident initially affected his eyes. They were wrapped with bandages for a couple of weeks. As I cared for him, we talked and got to know each other. I didn't know anything about that darn symbol on his arm," Elizabeth said. "I had no idea what it meant at the time. Long story short, we began to fall in love. When the bandages were removed, he was shocked to see I was biracial."

"That was my moment of truth," Jim said in a voice heavy with emotion. "Yes, it was a shocker, especially after all the stupid lies I'd swallowed for so long as a member of the AHN. But before me sat my heart and soul. The woman I'd fallen head over heels in love with. When I gazed into her beautiful eyes, I knew I was home. And that's when my life changed. God allowed me to live through that motorcycle accident for a reason. And I devoted the rest of my life to his message of love."

"We've had a wonderful life together," Elizabeth said, her eyes shimmering with tears.

"Heck, we have four grown children and seven grandchildren. I call them my rainbow of love," Jim pointed to the framed Christmas photo of his entire family. "Lizzy, show them our family."

Sister Maggie and Sister Mary Felicia looked at the photo and smiled. "Such a handsome family," said Sister Maggie.

"When Jim left the hospital, he courted me, we got engaged, married, and were disowned by the entire Wade family," Elizabeth said, holding her husband's hand. "We decided Indiana wasn't a good place for us to settle down, so we came back here to Florida. My husband retired from ARS Industrial Cleaning Supplies after working for the company as its plant manager for over forty years. Until last year, he actively led the Abundant Life Christian Church."

"I know you're here to learn about Calvin and Cody Pierce and not our love story or my work as a minister, but I wanted you to know that I was part of the AHN. I also needed you to know that people can change. If I could change, anyone can."

"Jim, tell them about your connection to Calvin and Cody," said Al.

"Well, those two are my first cousins. Yes, I was here on vacation at the time of my accident, but I was here to look for work, too. After I got out of the hospital, I got a job at ARS Industrial Cleaning Supplies and got my cousins Calvin and Cody jobs there too. At the time, I thought if I did something good for them, the family would accept Lizzy."

"And did they?"

Jim shook his head. "Of course not. My two younger cousins were also members of the AHN. They joined around the same time I did. Even after I got them jobs, they turned around and treated me like dirt. Just like the rest of my family, they wanted nothing to do with Lizzy and me or our kids. Even though we worked for the same company, we avoided each other like the plague," Jim said as he pursed his lips.

"I'm so sorry you went through that," Sister Mary Felicia said.

"Thank you, my dear, but it was so very long ago and we've made our peace with it," Lizzy said.

"I remember one time, early on in our marriage, Calvin and Cody both stopped by our house. Lizzy was pregnant with our daughter at the time, and she was tending the garden while the boys played in the yard. My cousins showed up out of the blue and started hurling insults at my wife and said our children were nothing more than mongrels. They threatened to hurt Lizzy and the baby. When Lizzy told me, I went to the president of the company, Ray Stanley, and asked him for a favor. I told him I wanted both men transferred out of Florida. Calvin was sent to Georgia, and Cody left the company altogether. This was after your twin disappeared," said Jim.

"Tell Sister Maggie what you told me back then," Lizzy said.

"Calvin and Cody were both bad news. They were not only racists filled with venomous hate, but they also enjoyed violence. All I know is that I instructed Lizzy to make sure she and our children were never alone with either one of them. When they left the state, we both breathed a sigh of relief."

"We never heard from them or saw them again," Lizzy said. "Calvin never married, but Cody did. That's all we know. I can tell you from my encounter with them in the front garden all those years ago that I'd never been so terrified in all my life. I scooped up my kids and ran inside the house and locked the door."

"Reverend Wade, can you tell us what your cousins looked like?" Sister Maggie asked.

"They looked a lot alike back then. They were brothers. They both had black curly hair and were about average height. Both were pretty slim too."

"Do you remember them being into sports or coaching a team?"

"We all played softball on the company team," Reverend Wade said. "Funny, you should ask about that. I remember both Calvin and Cody had wanted to try out for one of the minor baseball teams but when they saw there were a lot of African Americans trying out, they turned around and left."

The description of the man in Sister Maggie's visions certainly fit either of the two men. *Did one of them do it or were they both in on it?*

"Sister Maggie, I can tell you that at the time, we remembered reading about your sister and seeing it on the news, but I had no idea that my cousins might be involved. Considering their beliefs, it didn't even cross my mind that they would think of kidnapping a white girl. I never saw my cousins behaving strangely around girls or anything. But they could have hidden it. Forgive me, Sister Maggie, but the worst-case scenario was that it could have been an abduction motivated by sexual perversion. Back then, we didn't talk about pedophilia. I tell you, when folks say things were better back in the day, I disagree."

Sister Maggie took in a deep, shaky breath. "It was a horrible time for my family, especially thinking about what could have happened to Catie." Sister Maggie had wrestled with those thoughts for years, and the pain never went away.

"Sister Maggie, I can only imagine how hard it must have been on you and your family," Jim said. "But I can tell you this. When Al reached out to us, it all became clear to me. I realized it could indeed have been one or both of my cousins who abducted Catie."

CHAPTER THIRTY-ONE

May 22, 10:00 a.m.
McKinney Tunnel
Miami, Florida

CATIE, *where are you?*

Sister Maggie placed her hand on the concrete wall of the tunnel and closed her eyes. She recalled the letters "ey" in the name of the tunnel. They were standing in McKinney Tunnel on the narrow sidewalk. A fence ran along the entire length of the tunnel to keep pedestrians safe from the traffic speeding by. *Is this the place you showed me, Catie?* She hoped Catie would appear to her, but nothing happened. "Are you sure this is the tunnel? It had rocks that lined the walls back then," Sister Maggie said remembering the other part of her vision.

"This *was* the only tunnel in the area at the time your sister disappeared. I assure you," Al stressed. An SUV and two cars whooshed by them. "We should get back to my van since it's a busy road," he said in a louder voice, over the traffic noise.

Sister Maggie opened her eyes and turned around. Al and Sister Mary Felicia were watching her. Both wore the same expression on their face. Concern.

"Are you okay?" Sister Mary Felicia asked.

Sister Maggie nodded, crossing her arms in front of her. "When we were kids, Catie and I could finish each other's sentences and read each other's thoughts. That's the way with twins. We were best friends as well as sisters. The day she disappeared, a part of me died, too. Maybe, I've been trying to find that missing part ever since."

Sister Mary Felicia approached Sister Maggie in the tunnel. "Sister Maggie, we'll find out what happened to Catie. I know we will."

"I promise you, Sister Maggie, I will keep working on this," Al said.

"Thank you. Thank you both. I know we will," Sister Maggie said as she followed Al and Sister Mary Felicia out of the tunnel to Al's vehicle parked off the side of the road.

As they drove away to the airport, she watched as the tunnel disappeared from sight in the side-view mirror. She continued to stare out the passenger window as they passed a body of water. A jolt of awareness shot through her like an electric current. "Pull over, Al! Pull over!"

"Hold on," Al said as he put on his right-turn signal. He slowed down and brought the van to a full stop on the shoulder of the road.

Sister Maggie pointed to her right. "What body of water is that?"

"The Miami River," Al said.

"I need to get out of the van."

"Okay. Please be careful. Let's not have any highway accidents this morning, sisters," he cautioned as he watched the traffic from his side-view mirror.

Sister Maggie stood by the metal barrier that prevented cars from free-falling into the river. She stared out at the water. The ripples suggested it was home to a variety of fish. Although the river cut through downtown Miami, the area below was bordered by vegetation and weeds. A few palm trees and grass could be seen closer to the commercial development farther down the river. Sister Maggie could see many large homes beyond the commercial area.

"Al, what if my sister's body was dumped in the Miami River?"

Al walked up to the metal barrier beside Sister Maggie. "Although this water tends to be very polluted, her remains would have been discovered years ago," he said. "Parts of this river have been dredged numerous times since Catie's disappearance. What's more likely is the killer hid her body on dry land, especially if he didn't have a boat."

"Sister Maggie. Do you have a sense that your sister's death is somehow tied to this river?" asked Sister Mary Felicia.

Sister Maggie nodded. "Maybe he buried her where no one could find her."

"This area is massive," Al said. "And it's undergone vast commercial development over the past fifty years. With all the construction over the years, they would have found her remains."

"What about that residential area in the distance?" Sister Mary Felicia asked.

"That's the town of Madison Palms—actually more of a village. It's an older area."

"Maybe the killer drove by here with Catie in his car all those years ago. And she stared out at the same stretch of river we're looking at now."

"That's a possibility. But the next step is for you to speak with Cody Pierce. He might be the only one who can give you the answers you seek." Al glanced at his watch. "I'd better get the two of you to the airport."

Sister Maggie buckled her seat belt and stared blankly at the road. An image began to form in her mind. It wasn't like her dream visions but more like an inspirational thought. The image of a disheveled Catie standing in the unrenovated tunnel signaled to her that although dirtied and muddied, she wasn't soaking wet or drenched. Maybe she was still alive in that tunnel but was killed later on. Sister Maggie turned to Al. "When did they begin the tunnel renovation?"

"The tunnel was closed to traffic weeks before and months after Catie was kidnapped," Al replied.

"Catie must have been alive and terrorized by her killer while she was in or near this tunnel," Sister Maggie said barely above a whisper.

Al said. "We'll find the answer."

"Thank you, Al, for everything." Sister Maggie turned back to the window and watched the river as the van sped along the highway.

I promise Catie, we're going to bring you home one day.

CHAPTER THIRTY-TWO

June 5, 10:30 a.m.
Indianapolis, Indiana

"I HAVE SPOKEN with Dale Wells on numerous occasions, and I firmly believe that he is not guilty of willfully killing Sam Browning." Sister Maggie clasped her hands on her knees as she faced the courtroom.

"And how can you be sure of that, Sister Maggie?"

"He told me."

The courtroom erupted into a loud buzzing as the prosecuting attorney Laura Wilson stood. "Objection, your honor. This is hearsay. Sister Maggie Donovan cannot know the intention of the defendant Dale Wells at the moment the gun went off."

Sister Maggie addressed Laura Wilson and spoke to her in a calm voice. "Just as I swore to tell the whole truth when I laid my hand on the Bible here today, I tell you that I believe Dale Wells. The death of Sam Browning was a terrible tragedy, and it was also an accident. Dale confessed the truth to me and before God. Are you saying I'm lying?" Sister Maggie lifted an eyebrow and looked around the courtroom. Her glance took in the jury, Dale, Charlie, the lawyers, and a wide-eyed Sister Mary Felicia seated between Jaime and Jose, who were both grinning.

"Your honor," Laura Wilson addressed the judge. "This is highly inappropriate."

Judge Beverly Debussy cleared her throat and tapped her gavel as the spectators continued to chatter in the courtroom. "I will have order in this courtroom." She turned to the jury and explained the definition of hearsay once more. "While Sister Maggie Donovan is a respected member of the community and has sworn to tell us the truth, by law, we cannot accept her statement as fact."

Sometimes the law is wrong. Sister Maggie stepped down and walked to the back of the courtroom and resumed her seat beside Sister Mary Felicia.

"Sister Maggie, you're probably going to be all over the news for that," Sister Mary Felicia whispered.

"I only spoke the truth." Despite the judge instructing the jury to disregard her statement, she prayed that Deidre Browning would do the right thing. She'd bumped into Sam's mother in the women's washroom earlier. Deidre had confessed to Sister Maggie that her son had been guilt-ridden about his relationship with Charlie and how much he regretted complicating things for her and Dale. She also told Sister Maggie that Sam's father, her ex-husband, told her she'd be betraying Sam if she didn't testify that Sam feared for his life because of Dale's jealousy.

"Dale is the vet to my two dogs. How can such a gentle and caring vet be capable of cold-blooded murder? I don't believe he planned to kill Sam."

"You must answer the questions honestly. I'm sure, given the kind of person Sam was, he would have wanted you to tell the truth."

Deidre nodded as tears streamed down her face. "I was so happy when he transferred here from New York. I had thought he would never set foot back in Indiana after everything that happened when he was so young."

Sister Maggie's thoughts returned to the courtroom as the judge declared a recess for lunch. Jaime and Jose both had to get back to work, but Sister Maggie and Sister Mary Felicia waited to speak with Charlie, who stepped out into the hall and walked up to them.

"How is Dale doing?" Sister Maggie asked.

"He's meeting with David over lunch to go over a few things," Charlie said. She clutched her purse in front of her in a tight grip.

"Have faith," Sister Maggie said.

"Would you and Sister Mary Felicia pray for us today?"

"Of course, we will. Do you want us to stay with you until after the recess?"

"I'm going back in with Dale, but if you don't mind praying for us at the convent? Dale and I would be so grateful. We're going to need all the help we can get,"

"We will most certainly do that," Sister Maggie said with a firm nod.

"All the sisters will pray with us," Sister Mary Felicia added.

"Thank you so much. And thank you for believing in us—in Dale," Charlie said.

"How is he holding up?" Sister Maggie asked.

"He's doing well. He's changed over the past few weeks for the better. I can't remember when we've ever talked so much or shared so much about our childhoods and our hopes and dreams. In a strange way, this entire tragedy has brought us closer than we've ever been."

They hugged Charlie and returned to the convent, where they gathered with Sister Mary Frances, Sister Ruthie, and Sister Rose Marie. Once in the chapel, they knelt in their pews. Sister Maggie prayed out loud—"Lord, you know all things. Our past, present, and future are in your merciful hands. I pray now for Dale as he faces what could be a prison sentence or acquittal. Please give the judge and jury wisdom. And please give Dale and Charlie the strength to deal with the verdict no matter what happens."

CHAPTER THIRTY-THREE

June 5, 5:30 p.m.
Our Lady of Guadalupe Convent
New Hope, Indiana

"I'LL GET THE PHONE," Sister Mary Felicia said as she walked briskly from the chapel to the hallway phone following Evening Prayer.

Sisters Maggie, Ruthie, Mary Frances, and Rose Marie headed to the kitchen where roast chicken, rice, and brussels sprouts were warming in the oven.

"It may be news about Dale," Sister Maggie said. They had all agreed not to watch the TV news or go online to find out about his verdict.

Sister Mary Felicia had a look of horror on her face as she gestured for Sister Maggie to come to the phone. "It's Charlie. She wants us to meet her in the emergency room at the hospital."

"Charlie, what happened?" Sister Maggie asked as she put the phone to her ear.

"Sister Maggie, you have to get here as fast as you can. I don't think I can handle this by myself."

Sister Maggie shook her head as Charlie sketched out briefly what happened. "We'll be there as soon as possible." Sister Maggie hung up the phone and turned to the other sisters. "You'll have to have dinner without us. Sister Mary Felicia and I need to get to St. Barnabas Hospital in Indianapolis. The good news is that Dale was acquitted. The bad news is he was shot outside the courthouse!"

Forty-five minutes later, Sisters Maggie and Mary Felicia arrived at the emergency room of St. Barnabus Hospital.

"Look, there's Charlie with Jaime." Sister Mary Felicia pointed as they entered the waiting room.

"What's going on?" asked Sister Maggie. "How's Dale?"

Charlie blew her nose. Her eyes were red from crying. "Dale w-was holding my hand as we left the courthouse. Laura Wilson, the prosecutor, was just behind us. As we walked down the steps, we spotted Mitchel Fowler, who was ranting and raving. He started screaming at Laura. She was only a few feet behind us. Fowler cursed at her for not offering him a deal. He said he could have been the star witness in the case. He shouted even louder that the deal would have bought him some protection from the AHN, who had kicked him out and would most likely put a hit on him. Then he pulled a gun from his jacket and aimed it at Laura," Charlie said. She stared ahead as though witnessing the horror again.

Charlie gulped and continued. "Dale was the first to act. He tackled Fowler and wrestled him to the ground. My husband struggled with Fowler to try to get the gun away from him, and Fowler must have managed to pull the trigger, and the bullet hit Dale. Everything happened so fast. The courthouse police ran down the steps and grabbed Fowler before he got away. Luckily, an ambulance was already in the parking lot. It didn't take long for the paramedics to rush Dale here. I still don't know how badly he's wounded. When I called you earlier, they were prepping him for surgery," Charlie said.

Sister Maggie noticed that Charlie's color was off. She was paler than normal. "Why don't we sit down and wait together? Have you had anything to drink?"

Charlie shook her head.

"How about some tea or coffee?"

Charlie nodded. "Hot tea with sugar sounds good."

Jaime offered to get it and asked Sisters Maggie and Mary Felicia if they wanted something, but they both declined.

As Charlie sipped her hot tea, she shook her head. "I still can't believe it."

Sisters Maggie, Mary Felicia, and Jaime offered to pray a rosary for a successful surgery.

"Thank you," Charlie said and joined them in prayer.

By eight-thirty in the evening, the surgeon, Dr. Bennett, reappeared and headed in their direction.

"Your husband is one lucky guy," Dr. Bennett said. "The bullet went through his chest and missed his heart. One inch, either way, could have been fatal. Dale should make a full recovery."

The doctor looked over at the two sisters as they put their rosaries away.

"I guess there's something to be said for prayer," Dr. Bennett mused.

"Mitchel Fowler pulled the trigger, but God directed the angle of the bullet," Sister Maggie said confidently.

"Probably so. Probably so," Dr. Bennett said with arched eyebrows.

As the surgeon walked away, Charlie hugged Sister Maggie. This time Charlie's tears were those of joy. Jaime put his arm around Sister Mary Felicia and gave her a big hug.

Sister Maggie clutched her crucifix and silently prayed in thanksgiving for Dale's life as Charlie chatted with Jaime and Sister Mary Felicia. From the corner of her eye, Sister Maggie spotted a familiar figure standing at the entrance of the emergency room. It was Sam. The gunshot wound to his head was gone. He smiled and gave a little nod, then he turned and vanished in a flash of light.

May the souls of all the faithful departed, through the mercy of God, rest in peace.

EPILOGUE

July 10, 11:00 a.m.
St. Anne's Church
Indianapolis, Indiana

"I DO," Sister Maggie replied to Father Macias's question.

Sister Maggie lifted Daniel, the cherubic baby boy with thick black hair, so that Father Macias could sign the child on the forehead with the cross. Then Dale and Charlie did the same, and so did Sister Maggie and Dale's cousin Eduardo, who were the official godparents. Sister Maggie was thrilled when the adoption came through and honored that Dale and Charlie asked her to be godmother to their baby boy.

When the water was poured on Daniel's head, he opened his big brown eyes and began to giggle, much to everyone's amazement, including Father Macias.

After the ceremony, they all returned to Dale and Charlie's home for a celebration.

"Why the name Daniel?" asked Sister Maggie as Charlie cuddled her little boy on her lap on the living room couch. Daniel was still wrapped in his white blanket and slept soundly tucked into the crook of her arm. "I thought you were going to name him Dale."

"Ask my husband," replied Charlie as Dale and his mother Maria Rosales-Wells walked up to them.

Maria smiled. "Dale is a very Anglo name. Of course, I wanted to honor my husband, so on the birth certificate, his name is Dale, but I decided to call him Danilo. It's also a Spanish form of Daniel."

"Speaking of Spanish, the food smells delicious," Sister Maggie said.

"It's a Colombian specialty soup called *sancocho*," Maria said. The soup contained various meats and fish with large pieces of cassava and vegetables, including corn and cilantro. "And, it's almost ready," Maria added, with a twinkle in her eye. "I'll be right back." She leaned over and kissed her grandson's head and then hurried to the kitchen, gesturing to Sisters Ruthie, Mary Frances, and Rose Marie. The trio had also been on kitchen duty helping to prepare the food for the baptism celebration.

Sister Ruthie had baked apple and peach pies, while Sister Mary Frances had made fried chicken and Swedish meatballs, and Sister Rose Marie had made oven-baked potatoes with roasted vegetables, and a Caesar salad.

A few minutes later, they all gathered around the dining room table, and Father Macias said grace. Sister Maggie looked around the table at all the friends, both old and new, who'd joined in the celebration. Sister Mary Felicia, Jaime Bauer, Bob Souter, Travis Campbell, Jose and Marisol Torres, David Moore—Dale's defense lawyer, and Laura Wilson—the prosecuting attorney—who were both now dating.

Despite Laura's role as a prosecutor in his case, Dale came to respect her determination to get to the truth. After she visited him in the hospital following the shooting at the courthouse—and knowing he had saved her life—they developed a genuine friendship that embraced Charlie as well. When Laura adopted a rescue dog, their friendship deepened as Dale and Charlie personally helped Laura to train Rufus.

Sister Maggie smiled at the change in Dale over the past months.

As Mama Lulu always said, *If life doesn't kill you, it makes you stronger and more resilient.*

Sister Maggie was proud of Sister Mary Felicia and Jaime. They had testified at Mitch Fowler's trial and helped convict him of his crimes. Among them were attempted murder, trafficking stolen weapons and goods, and distributing illegal drugs. Like Frank King and Dylan King, the only sunlight Fowler would see for the rest of his life was outside in the prison yard at specified times.

Sister Mary Felicia piped up, "The *sancocho* is delicious."

"My mother-in-law loves to cook, and Dale and I love to eat," said Charlie. "It's a win-win situation. We've asked Maria to move in with us. We have a separate in-law suite for Maria. She can still have her privacy and Daniel will have his *abuelita* to care for him while I work part-time with Leo, and Dale resumes his work at the animal clinic," said Charlie.

Maria pinched her grandson's cheek as he drank his milk. She spoke to him in Spanish. "*Mira, el entiende todo.*"

"Maria will also be teaching me Spanish," Charlie said as she lifted Daniel to a sitting position and adjusted his white baptism outfit. "Who knows, I may even teach Leo some Spanish. He'll be the first bilingual ape in Indiana, maybe even in the world."

Travis had spoken a few moments in private with Sister Maggie earlier and told her Leo had signed to him that Papa-Sam was "asleep". The orangutan had come to terms with the fact that Sam was not returning. Sister Maggie told Travis that she and Sister Mary Felicia would be stopping by for a visit soon and a little impromptu concert for Leo.

"We might even sneak in a meat-cheese-bread," she'd told him.

"I heard that." Bob Souter had cleared his throat behind them, and everyone had had a good laugh.

The newly minted godfather Eduardo, or Eddie as everyone called him, and his wife Gabriella chatted animatedly with Sister Mary Felicia about music. Both had excellent singing voices and were choir members at St. Anne Parish. They began sharing their knowledge of contemporary Christian music, especially popular Spanish songs.

"I wonder if I should include a few Christian songs in Spanish on my record album," Sister Mary Felicia said.

"*Por supuesto*!" Eddie and Gabriella responded. "Of course!"

Sister Mary Felicia told the couple she would be in touch with them. She even suggested their entire church choir could be featured as backup singers on the Spanish songs.

Sister Maggie marveled at the relationships forming around her. She noted that if it were not for Leo, the orangutan, she would never have met Charlie, Dale, Maria, Eddie, and Gabriella. More important, the adorable little boy named Daniel, her godchild, would not be in her life.

She was also thankful for Mel Gonzales-Mendez and Al Reyes who were helping her track down Catie's killer. After Al informed her Cody Pierce was living at the Sisters of Elderly Sick in Brooklyn, Sister Maggie had promptly contacted her dear friend Sister Mary Grace to help her set up a visit. Sister Mary Grace knew the director of the nursing home very well. Unfortunately, Sister Maggie had to wait a while longer to speak to Cody, as he was ill with pneumonia. It seemed like every time she took a step forward in her sister's cold case, she ended up falling two steps back. But she would not give up. She would never give up.

Charlie handed Daniel to Sister Maggie so she could grab a bite to eat. Sister Maggie kissed Daniel on the forehead and he snuggled his head against her white scapular as he fell asleep.

"Sleep, little boy. You have a lot of growing to do and many adventures ahead of you," whispered Sister Maggie. She thought of all that had happened to deliver the small child here. "You've traveled a long way to be with your new family," Sister Maggie said. Daniel opened his eyes and regarded her with a curious expression. "You're going to have a wonderful life. I just know it. Your loving family watching over you in Heaven and your loving family watching over you here." She tapped his nose with a gentle finger, and he began to gurgle and giggle and then abruptly spat up milk on Sister Maggie's white scapular.

"At least it's whitish on white," joked Sister Mary Felicia as Sister Maggie spot-cleaned her scapular with a cloth napkin.

"You seemed lost in thought," said Sister Mary Felicia later. She held Daniel while Sister Maggie dabbed at her scapular in the kitchen.

"I was thinking about the journey of life," said Sister Maggie.

"Oh, dear," said Sister Mary Felicia, as she dramatically placed the back of her hand on her forehead. "I feel a deep philosophical or theological monologue coming on."

Sister Maggie wagged her finger at the cheeky young nun. "Think about it. We live moment to moment, day to day, yet we never witness our humble beginning and try to put off the inevitable—our end. It's God who sees our entire life all at once. There is no mystery for God —no moment to moment or day to day. Our loving God is timeless and eternal," Sister Maggie said.

"All this because the baby spit up on you?"

Sister Maggie smiled. "Seriously, I've been thinking a lot about time and eternity. Somehow Catie's death always forces me to see beyond this world to eternity. God willing, I will enter the heavenly kingdom one day and be reunited with Catie. I suppose knowing Catie's killer won't matter much after that, but it matters now," Sister Maggie stressed. "Catie was and is such an important part of who I am. More than anything, I want to honor her by giving her a proper Christian burial. She deserves it. I want her remains consigned to sacred ground."

Sister Maggie noticed that Daniel lifted his hand in the air as he slept. She gently took hold of it and kissed the back of it.

"Life may be mysterious, but divine love has a way of reaching out to us and allowing us to experience unconditional love in our lifetime. Imagine the impossible—the incredible—the boundless nature of that same divine love filling us with joy."

"Sister Maggie, we don't have to wait to get to Heaven to experience the boundless love of God," Charlie said as she overheard Sister Maggie. She and Dale strolled into the kitchen. "It starts in this life. We were going to tell everyone later after we served the cake, but we want you both to know now. Dale and I are happy to announce that we're expecting again."

"Congratulations," Sister Maggie and Sister Mary Felicia both exclaimed. Sister Mary Felicia handed the gurgling Daniel to Dale.

"Tell them about your father," Charlie said to Dale.

Dale nodded. "My mother reminded me during the trial that I must never lose hope. She told me that on my father's deathbed, despite my father's profound failings as a husband and father, he knew that he had to humble himself and ask for my forgiveness for his sins. He realized too late that his actions had crippled me emotionally. When I refused to forgive him before he passed away, he told my mother he would accept my refusal as a just punishment for his infidelities," Dale paused. "During my darkest day, when I had actually considered suicide, my father came to me in a dream. He called out to me, 'Danny boy, what you're contemplating is unspeakable. To throw away your life as though it were a piece of trash would be an eternal shame. I love you, son.' I woke up and knew in the depths of my soul that my father spoke to me from the grave. It was at that moment I forgave him. For the first time, I felt redeemed again."

Sister Maggie nodded. "We can be frivolous and waste our days, choose not to love, and reject the good. But embracing love and goodness creates the seeds of our redemption." Sister Maggie believed that down to the depths of her soul. Even with criminals like Fowler, the Kings, and the rest of the AHN, and yes, even with Catie's murderer, redemption was possible.

DEAR READER...

Thank you for reading ***Sworn to Murder***, Book 2 in the Sister Maggie Mystery Series.
I hope you are enjoying getting to know Sister Maggie, her family, and friends.

Please take a moment to give ***Sworn to Murder*** a review. Reviews help authors tremendously, even sisters like me!

Please go to **Amazon.com** to leave a review.

You can download and share the fun and colorful cover for ***Sworn to Murder***, created by **Mystery Cover Designs**, on Pinterest, Instagram, or another social media site.

Blessings,
Sister Diane Carollo
P.S. Keep reading for a sneak peek of my next book!

SNEAK PEEK

SR. DIANE CAROLLO

A Vow of Murder

A Sister Maggie Mystery
Book 3

sisterdianecarollo.com

August 18, 3:30 p.m.
North Willow Senior Assisted Living
Douglaston, Queens

"Mom, did Dad ever talk to you about the Mafia when he was in the NYPD? Was he ever asked to serve as an undercover agent to get to the bosses or capos?" Sister Maggie asked as she folded the article from the *New York Daily Herald* she'd been reading about the legacy of organized crime in New York.

Lulu glanced up from her crossword and shook her head. "You're so melodramatic, dear. Your father never went undercover to arrest mobsters or anyone else. You've watched too many police shows. Anyway, going undercover would have been very unwise since your dad knew many of the Mafia families in Brooklyn and Queens. More importantly, *they* knew the Donovans."

"You and Dad never talked about them?" Sister Maggie probed.

"Your dad grew up in Brooklyn and had several close friends that came from families with strong ties to the Mafia. Despite going into law enforcement, he maintained his friendships with many of the guys who came from those families," Lulu added.

"Dad was always a man committed to law and order. How did he reconcile being in the NYPD and having relationships with people who were involved in criminal activities?"

"Now did I say they were all criminals?" Lulu countered. "Listen, some of his friends came from Mafia families, but they didn't all go into the family business as adults."

"You and Dad certainly grew up in an interesting time," Sister Maggie said, raising her eyebrows.

"Maureen do you remember Mario Russo and his wife, Angela,

who used to visit us in Queens when you and Red were little?" asked Lulu. Her voice hitched as she spoke. "Did I ever tell you that Mario reached out to your dad after Catie's disappearance and offered to help?"

"Yes, I remember you telling us." Sister Maggie, whose given name was Maureen, reached out and wrapped her hands around her mother's. They closed their eyes and remembered Sister Maggie's identical red-headed twin who was abducted from an amusement park in Miami during a family vacation on spring break over fifty years ago. Decades later, memories of Catie still evoked feelings of sadness, guilt, and anger for Lulu, Sister Maggie, and the rest of the Donovan clan. The hardest thing to deal with was the fact that Catie's body had never been recovered or put to rest in sacred ground.

Sister Maggie was hoping to rectify that soon. She was staying with Lulu for a couple of days before her upcoming visit at the Sisters of the Elderly Sick in Brooklyn to talk to Cody Pierce, a man who may have been involved in Catie's abduction and murder. Sister Maggie had traveled to Miami in May to meet with Al Reyes, a private investigator who was looking into Catie's disappearance. Al had narrowed it down to two brothers—Calvin and Cody Pierce. Unfortunately, Calvin died of a drug overdose in Atlanta a few months back.

Sister Maggie had contacted her childhood friend and Superior General, Sister Mary Grace to help smooth the way for her to speak with Cody. He was now living at the nursing home of the Sisters of the Elderly Sick. Sister Mary Grace and Mother Frances Cecilia, the director of the home, were friends.

It had been a waiting game for Sister Maggie to be granted access due to Cody's precarious health. He'd been battling through a bout of pneumonia for weeks, after undergoing treatment for mouth cancer. Then last week, Sister Mary Grace phoned Sister Maggie to let her know that Calvin was doing better and Mother Frances Cecilia was allowing a visit. Sister Mary Grace, who was also back in New York, would be going with her. The two friends agreed that Lulu should not be told about the upcoming visit. Past disappoints and dead-end leads might be too much for the elderly woman. Only Sister Maggie's younger brother Johnny and his wife Eileen knew what was going on and had promised to keep it under wraps.

Sister Maggie stepped into Lulu's kitchenette and brewed a pot of coffee. Opening the fridge, she took out the white box containing an assortment of Italian pastries she'd purchased that morning from *Biscotti di Nonna,* the Italian bakery around the corner. Sister Maggie had tried to resist, but in the end, she'd given in and purchased a half-dozen of the delectable treats. She took out a cannoli for herself and a slice of lemon ricotta cake for Lulu and poured two cups of freshly brewed coffee. Placing everything on a tray, Sister Maggie carried it out to the living room and set the tray down on the coffee table.

"Was Mario in the Mafia?" Sister Maggie asked a few minutes later, after they'd indulged their sweet tooths.

"Mario steered his life away from the Mafia." Lulu sighed, wiping her mouth with a napkin. "I know his son Tony is okay, but I don't know about his other son Phil.

"Refresh my memory about their heritage," Sister Maggie said, taking a sip of her coffee.

"Well, Mario's father, Anthony Russo, immigrated to America with his parents from Sicily when Anthony was ten years old. Anthony grew up in a different time. Unfortunately, he ended up in the Mafia but he didn't want that for his son Mario or his daughters, so he opened a restaurant in Manhattan in a very chic area, away from the mob's influence. He named it after Mario's grandmother, Maria. It ended up doing amazing business and began the Russo family's journey to becoming legit. And the rest as they say is history."

"Ah, yes, I remember you telling me the origins of Mama Maria's," Sister Maggie said. Sister Maggie and her family had eaten there many times over the years. She recalled Lulu mentioning that Mario's second son Tony took it over when Mario retired for health reasons. Tony expanded the business into one of the most popular Italian restaurant chains in New York and New Jersey.

"Mario was your father's good friend," Lulu added. "Just because he came from a Mafia family didn't mean he was no good. He and his wife Angela were also very charitable as you know."

"Yes, they were, they both left a generous donation to the Adorers of Devine Love when they passed," agreed Sister Maggie. "Mario and Angela had three sons and a daughter, right?"

"Mario Junior was the eldest, then Tony who was named after Anthony, the grandfather, then Tina, and the youngest was Filippo named after Angela's father, but everyone calls him Phil," Lulu said. "Mario and Angela were heartbroken when Mario Junior died in Afghanistan. Mario and Angela were so proud of him when he joined the Marines after college, but they worried all the time. After 9/11 he was deployed to Afghanistan and killed in action. Such a tragedy."

"Yes, I remember Mario and Angela weren't the same after that," Sister Maggie said.

"They were devastated. Angela said to me a few months after the funeral—'Lulu, now I truly understand what you go through every day after you lost Catie.'" Lulu wiped her eyes with a tissue then picked up the newspaper article and scanned through the story.

Sister Maggie's heart broke every time her mother cried about Catie. Trying to shift her mother's mind in another direction Sister Maggie said, "Mom, you were raised in Brooklyn, just blocks away from the Donovans. Did you know anyone in the Mafia when you were growing up? As an Italian American, it would make more sense for you to have been more knowledgeable of the Mafia than Daddy, who was just one generation removed from Ireland."

Lulu folded the newspaper and set it aside. "We knew a few of the Mafia families in Brooklyn, but Grandpa Fred D'Amico kept his distance from them. He might have been worried that one of his three daughters would marry into one of the crime families," Lulu joked.

"So, you never dated anyone from the Mafia?" Sister Maggie asked with a smile.

"My first and only love was your dear father. John and I knew each other since we were children. We became high school sweethearts. We often socialized with some of your father's friends who came from Mafia families. They weren't all bad," Lulu added.

"I know Mom," Sister Maggie said. "Dad used to say—they are three types of criminals—those who commit crimes out of desperation, those who commit crimes for money or profit, and those who commit crimes because they are evil."

"I know the kind of criminal who abducted Catie all those years ago," Lulu whispered.

Sister Maggie sighed and wrapped her arm around her mother's frail shoulders. Lulu was right—the man who abducted Catie fifty years ago *was* evil. There was no other explanation for it. Sister Maggie prayed Cody Pierce could lead her to the truth, so the Donovans could finally bring Catie home.

Dear Reader...

I hope you enjoyed this little sneak peek of ***A Vow of Murder***, Book 3 in the Sister Maggie Mystery Series.

Please visit sisterdianecarollo.com to sign up for my newsletter and find out more about ***A Vow of Murder*** as well as other future releases and upcoming events.

Blessings,
Sister Diane Carollo

ABOUT THE AUTHOR

Sister Diane Carollo, S.G.L., earned a master's degree in Biblical Studies at Providence College in Rhode Island. Originally from Brooklyn, New York, she has served as a religious among the poor at St. Brigid Parish in New York City, St Malachy Parish in Brooklyn, New York, and in the Mission and Vocations Offices for the Archdiocese of Newark, New Jersey. For twelve years she served in the Archdiocese of Indianapolis, Indiana, as director of the Office for Pro-Life Ministry and as the part-time religious education director at Holy Rosary Parish in Indianapolis. Since June 2012, she has assumed the role of director of religious education at St. Luke the Evangelist Parish in Indianapolis.

Sister Diane began writing fiction in elementary school but gave it up to pursue other adventures when she spooked her teacher after writing a horror story for a class assignment. After that, Diane's mother sat her down for a chat—something she did from time to time —and suggested that Diane might consider writing, "happy and nice stories."

Now, forty years later, Sister Diane is once again writing stories—having found the perfect balance between "horror" and "happy and nice" in the form of the cozy mystery! A life-long avid fiction reader, and a fan of mystery novels, Sister Diane has written her debut mystery novel featuring an intrepid sleuth on a quest for justice—who also happens to be a nun. *Devoted to Murder* is the first book in the Sister Maggie Mystery Series.

Growing up in Brooklyn, New York, and working among the poor as a religious sister in some of the most crime-ridden areas in New York, Sister Diane realized that there is often a very fine line between truth and fiction. The plots for the Sister Maggie Mystery Series are borne not only from her imagination but inspired in part from actual life experiences.

When she's not writing or running religious education at St. Luke's, Sister Diane is usually tucked into a good book while trying not to chuckle at Courtney the cat's antics. Yes, there is an actual Courtney the cat, and the real one is just as mischievous as the fictional one who lives at the convent with Sister Maggie and the other sisters.

You can reach Sister Diane Carollo and sign up for her newsletter at sisterdianecarollo.com.
And you can also follow her on Amazon and BookBub.

Made in the USA
Monee, IL
25 May 2021